*"The Watsons by Jane A*         *....mpleted by Merryn
Williams is written in the style of Jane Austen. She is true
to the work of Jane Austen, and follows the story's continuation as originally described by Jane to Cassandra. The
story is gentle, the characters are developed through the story,
it is not padded to extend over several extraneous chapters,
and provides a very enjoyable reading experience. I enjoyed
it!"*

**Jane Austen Society, UK Membership Secretary**

*"We enjoyed it and are selling it!"*

**Jane Austen House Museum, UK**

*"I am happy that Merryn Williams has satisfied my
curiosity as to 'what happened next'. Her continuation of
The Watsons is as seamless as one might expect, although
her language is more friendly to 21st century readers. I liked
as well the plot-driven flow of the narrative towards a conclusion I found satisfying, very much in the spirit of Jane
Austen herself."*

**Jane Austen Society,
North America & Canada**

*"An engaging completion of The Watsons, and one of
the more seamless transitions from Austen's uncompleted
novel that I have read. I was glad to see that the character
of Emma was not materially altered, and that Emma is a*

*positive catalyst for change in her sister, Elizabeth, who grows from being a maudlin spinster to a woman with hope. We will never have the perfect completion of The Watsons, for we can never have Austen's completion. But this completion is particularly gratifying."*

**Lynn Lamy, Committee Member of**
**The Republic of Pemberley**

# *THE WATSONS*

by
Jane Austen

completed by
Merryn Williams

Pen Press Publishers Ltd

The Watsons written by
Jane Austen
was left unfinished and unpublished
at the time of her death in 1817

First published in Great Britain by
Indepenpress an imprint of
Pen Press Publishers Ltd
39 Chesham Road
Brighton
East Sussex BN2 1NB

ISBN 1-904754-93-7

Printed and bound in the UK

A catalogue record of this book is available from
the British Library

Cover design by Jacqueline Abromeit

## *Dedication*

My part of the book is dedicated to my
father-in-law, William Spooner Hemp (1916-2003)
and to my mother-in-law Dilys.

# THE
# WATSONS

## Prologue

The Reverend Henry Watson, of Stanton in the county of Surrey, was a man whose many good qualities had never won him the position he deserved. His living was small and poor, and his wife died after a short illness leaving him with six children; the eldest, Robert, a schoolboy of eighteen, and the youngest, Emma, a girl of barely five. All the neighbourhood said that the family must now live with the strictest economy, and that the four girls could hardly hope to be sought in marriage by men of their own rank. But help came, from a sister of Mrs Watson's who had for ten years been married to a gentleman with a fine estate in Shropshire, Mr Turner. This aunt, childless herself, was anxious to do anything she could for her sister's children. The Turners came at once to the bereaved family, putting up in the White Hart at D., and it ended with their offering to take the little Emma home with them and bring her up in all respects as their own.

Mr Watson hesitated, but not for long. He wished, but he could not think it right to keep his youngest child with him, as he had perfect confidence in the kindness of Mr and Mrs Turner and believed that they would eventually leave her eight or nine thousand pounds. Robert, who was then about to start work as a clerk, warmly seconded the plan. 'Emma will be off our hands for good', he said, 'and she will be an heiress'.

So Emma was carried off to Shropshire, over a hundred miles away, and for fourteen years saw almost nothing of her family, as Mr Watson was too poor and too busy to travel, and

Mr Turner had long been in indifferent health. The eldest daughter Elizabeth, a girl of fifteen when her mother died, became her father's housekeeper and the family somehow survived on its slender income. Meanwhile Emma lived on the most affectionate terms with her aunt and uncle, who educated her carefully and gave her every rational pleasure they could procure. She heard of Robert's marriage, of Sam's apprenticeship to a medical man in Guildford, but she could scarcely recall their faces or voices after so long a separation. At seventeen she lost her truest friend when Mr Turner died, but there seemed no reason why she and her aunt should not go on as they were for several years.

Mrs Turner grieved bitterly, but perhaps not very deeply. She had always loved society and been long deprived of it, and two years after her widowhood took her niece to a ball in a grand house near Ludlow. She herself, she said, could never expect to be happy again, but her dear Emma must not be deprived of the pleasures of youth. Yet it was the aunt, and not the niece, whose fate was decided at this ball. Captain O'Brien, an Irish gentleman spending his leave with Shropshire friends, was introduced to Mrs Turner and immediately made himself agreeable to her. In the shortest possible space of time they were married and the Captain, recalled to his regiment in Dublin, naturally expected to be accompanied by his new wife.

Emma had thought that she should be of the party. She could not like the man; she was distressed that her aunt, at her time of life and so soon after the loss of an excellent husband, should rush into marriage with one who was almost a stranger, but could only pray that she would be happy in her chosen lot. Her neighbours, less charitable, were of the opinion that Mrs Turner had run mad. As soon as his objective was gained, Captain O'Brien let go his charming manners and showed a hardness and roughness which shocked both women. He did not want his wife's niece to come to Ireland; she was only a niece and not a daughter; she had a family of her own who could very well provide for her. As for the fortune which she should have had one day, that was now his and not hers.

So Emma was sent home to the vicarage at Stanton, where she found everything much changed.

# Chapter One

THE FIRST WINTER assembly in the town of D. in Surrey[1] was to be held on Tuesday, October the thirteenth, and it was generally expected to be a very good one; a long list of country families was confidently run over as sure of attending, and sanguine hopes were entertained that the Osbornes themselves would be there.

The Edwardses' invitation to the Watsons followed of course. The Edwardses were people of fortune who lived in the town and kept their coach; the Watsons inhabited a village about three miles distant, were poor and had no close carriage; and ever since there had been balls in the place, the former were accustomed to invite the latter to dress, dine and sleep at their house, on every monthly return throughout the winter.

On the present occasion, as only two of Mr Watson's children were at home, and one was always necessary as companion to himself, for he was sickly and had lost his wife, one only could profit by the kindness of their friends. Miss Emma Watson, who was very recently returned to her family from the care of an aunt who had brought her up, was to make her first public appearance in the neighbourhood; and her eldest sister, whose delight in a ball was not lessened by a ten years' enjoyment, had some merit in cheerfully undertaking to drive her and all her finery in the old chair to D. on the important morning.

As they splashed along the dirty lane Miss Watson thus instructed and cautioned her inexperienced sister:

'I dare say it will be a very good ball, and among so many officers, you will hardly want partners. You will find Mrs Edwards' maid very willing to help you, and I would advise you to ask Mary Edwards's opinion if you are at all at a loss, for she has very good taste. If Mr Edwards does not lose his money at cards, you will stay as late as you can wish for; if he does, he will hurry you home perhaps, but you are sure of some comfortable soup. I hope you will be in good looks. I should not be surprised if you were to be thought one of the prettiest girls in the room, there is a great deal in novelty. Perhaps Tom Musgrave may take notice of you, but I would advise you by all means not to give him any encouragement. He generally pays attention to every new girl, but he is a great flirt and never means anything serious.'

'I think I have heard you speak of him before,' said Emma. 'Who is he?'

'A young man of very good fortune, quite independent, and remarkably agreeable, a universal favourite wherever he goes. Most of the girls hereabouts are in love with him, or have been. I believe I am the only one among them that have escaped with a whole heart, and yet I was the first he paid attention to, when he came into this country, six years ago; and very great attention indeed did he pay me. Some people say that he has never seemed to like any girl so well since, though he is always behaving in a particular way to one or another.'

'And how came *your* heart to be the only cold one?' said Emma, smiling.

'There was a reason for that,' replied Miss Watson, changing colour. 'I have not been very well used, Emma, among them; I hope you will have better luck.'

'Dear sister, I beg your pardon, if I have unthinkingly given you pain.'

'When first we knew Tom Musgrave,' continued Miss Watson without seeming to hear her, 'I was very much attached to a young man of the name of Purvis, a particular friend of Robert's, who used to be with us a great deal. Everybody thought it would have been a match.'

A sigh accompanied these words, which Emma respected in silence, but her sister after a short pause went on: 'You will naturally ask why it did not take place, and why he is married to another woman, while I am still single. But you must ask him – not me – and you must ask Penelope. Yes, Emma, Penelope was at the bottom of it all. She thinks everything fair for a husband; I trusted her, she set him against me, with a view of gaining him herself, and it ended in his discontinuing his visits and soon after marrying somebody else. Penelope makes light of her conduct, but *I* think such treachery very bad. It has been the ruin of my happiness. I shall never love any man as I loved Purvis. I do not think Tom Musgrave should be named with him in the same day.'

'You quite shock me by what you say of Penelope,' said Emma. 'Could a sister do such a thing? Rivalry, treachery between sisters! I shall be afraid of being acquainted with her – but I hope it was not so. Appearances were against her—'

'You do not know Penelope. There is nothing she would not do to get married – she would as good as tell you so herself. Do not trust her with any secrets of your own, take warning by me, do not trust her. She has her good qualities, but she has no faith, no honour, no scruples, if she can promote her own advantage. I wish with all my heart she was well married. I declare I had rather have her well married than myself.'

'Than yourself! Yes, I can suppose so. A heart, wounded like yours, can have little inclination for matrimony.'

'Not much indeed – but you know we must marry. I could do very well single for my own part. A little company, and a pleasant ball now and then, would be enough for me, if one could be young forever, but my father cannot provide for us, and it is very bad to grow old and be poor and laughed at. I have lost Purvis, it is true, but very few people marry their first loves. I should not refuse a man because he was not Purvis. Not that I can ever quite forgive Penelope.'

Emma shook her head in acquiescence.

'Penelope however has had her troubles,' continued Miss Watson; 'she was sadly disappointed in Tom Musgrave, who afterwards transferred his attentions from me to her, and whom she was very fond of; but he never means anything serious, and when he had trifled with her long enough, he began to slight her for Margaret, and poor Penelope was very wretched. And since then, she has been trying to make some match at Chichester; she won't tell us with whom, but I believe it is a rich old Dr Harding,[2] uncle to the friend she goes to see, and she has taken a vast deal of trouble about him and given up a great deal of time to no purpose as yet. When she went away the other day she said it should be the last time. I suppose you did not know what her particular business was at Chichester, nor guess at the object that could take her away from Stanton, just as you were coming home after so many years' absence.'

'No, indeed, I had not the smallest suspicion of it. I considered her engagement to Mrs Shaw just at that time as very unfortunate for me. I had hoped to find all my sisters at home, to be able to make an immediate friend of each.'

'I suspect the doctor to have had an attack of the asthma, and that she was hurried away on that account – the Shaws are quite on her side. At least I believe so, but she tells me nothing. She professes to keep her own counsel; she says, and truly enough, that "too many cooks spoil the broth".'

'I am sorry for her anxieties,' said Emma, 'but I do not like her plans or her opinions. I shall be afraid of her. She must have too masculine and bold a temper. To be so bent on marriage – to pursue a man merely for the sake of situation – is a sort of thing that shocks me; I cannot understand it. Poverty is a great evil, but to a woman of education and feeling it ought not, it cannot be the greatest. I would rather be a teacher at a school (and I can think of nothing worse) than marry a man I did not like.'

'I would rather do anything than be a teacher at a school,' said her sister. '*I* have been at school, Emma, and know what a life they lead; *you* never have. I should not like marrying a disagreeable man any more than yourself, but I do not think there *are* very many disagreeable men; I think I could like any good-humoured man with a comfortable income. I suppose my aunt brought you up to be rather refined.'

'Indeed, I do not know. My conduct must tell you how I have been brought up. I am no judge of it myself. I cannot compare my aunt's method with any other person's, because I know no other.'

'But I can see in a great many things that you are very refined. I have observed it ever since you came home, and I am afraid it will not be for your happiness. Penelope will laugh at you very much.'

'*That* will not be for my happiness, I am sure. If my opinions are wrong, I must correct them – if they are above my situation, I must endeavour to conceal them. But I doubt whether ridicule... Has Penelope much wit?'

'Yes, she has great spirits, and never cares what she says.'

'Margaret is more gentle, I imagine?'

'Yes – especially in company; she is all gentleness and mildness when anybody is by. But she is a little fretful and perverse among ourselves. Poor creature! she is possessed with the notion of Tom Musgrave's being more seriously in love with her than he ever was with anybody else, and is always expecting him to come to the point. This is the second time within this twelvemonth that she has gone to spend a month with Robert and Jane on purpose to egg him on by her absence – but I am sure she is mistaken, and that he will no more follow her to Croydon now than he did last March. He will never marry unless he can marry somebody very great; Miss Osborne, perhaps, or something in that style.'

'Your account of this Tom Musgrave, Elizabeth, gives me very little inclination for his acquaintance.'

'You are afraid of him. I do not wonder at you.'

'No, indeed – I dislike and despise him.'

'Dislike and despise Tom Musgrave! No, *that* you never can. I defy you not to be delighted with him if he takes notice of you. I hope he will dance with you – and I daresay he will, unless the Osbornes come with a large party, and then he will not speak to anybody else.'

'He seems to have most engaging manners!' said Emma. 'Well, we shall see how irresistible Mr Tom Musgrave and I find each other. I suppose I shall know him as soon as I enter the ballroom; he *must* carry some of his charm in his face.'

'You will not find him in the ballroom, I can tell you. You will go early that Mrs Edwards may get a good place by the fire, and he never comes till late; and if the Osbornes are coming, he will wait in the passage, and come in with them. I should like to look in upon you, Emma. If it was but a good day with my father, I would wrap myself up, and James should drive me over, as soon as I had made tea for him, and I should be with you by the time the dancing began.'

'What! would you come late at night, in this chair?'

'To be sure I would. There, I said you were very refined – and *that's* an instance of it.'

Emma for a moment made no answer; then at last she said: 'I wish, Elizabeth, you had not made a point of my going to this ball; I wish you were going instead of me. Your pleasure would be greater than mine. I am a stranger here, and know nobody but the Edwardses; my enjoyment therefore must be very doubtful. Yours, among all your acquaintance, would be certain. It is not too late to change. Very little apology could be requisite to the Edwardses, who must be more glad of your company than of mine, and I should most readily return to my father, and should not be at all afraid to drive this quiet old creature home. Your clothes I would undertake to find means of sending to you.'

'My dearest Emma,' cried Elizabeth warmly, 'do you think I would do such a thing? Not for the universe – but I shall never forget your good nature in proposing it. You must have a sweet temper indeed; I never met with anything like it! And would you really give up the ball, that I might be able to go to it? Believe me, Emma, I am not so selfish as that comes to. No, though I am nine years older than you are, I would not be the means of keeping you from being seen. You are very pretty, and it would be very hard that you should not have as fair a chance as we have all had to make your fortune. No, Emma, whoever stays at home this winter, it shan't be you. I am sure I should never have forgiven the person who had kept me from a ball at nineteen.'

Emma expressed her gratitude, and for a few minutes they jogged on in silence. Elizabeth first spoke.

'You will take notice who Mary Edwards dances with?'

'I will remember her partners if I can, but you know they will be all strangers to me.'

'Only observe whether she dances with Captain Hunter more than once; I have my fears in that quarter. Not that her father and mother like officers, but if she does, you know, it is all over with poor Sam. And I have promised to write him word who she dances with.'

'Is Sam attached to Miss Edwards?'

'Did not you know *that*?'

'How should I know it? How should I know in Shropshire what is passing of that nature in Surrey? It is not likely that circumstances of such delicacy should make any part of the scanty communication which passed between you and me for the last fourteen years.'

'I wonder I never mentioned it when I wrote. Since you have been at home, I have been so busy with my poor father and our great wash that I have had no leisure to tell you anything – but indeed I concluded you knew it all. Sam has been very much in love with her these two years, and it is a great disappointment to him that he cannot always get away to our balls, but Mr Curtis won't often spare him, and just now it is a sickly time at Guildford.'

'Do you suppose Miss Edwards inclined to like him?'

'I am afraid not. You know she is an only child, and will have at least ten thousand pounds.'

'But still she may like our brother.'

'Oh, no! The Edwardses look much higher. Her father and mother would never consent to it. Sam is only a surgeon, you know. Sometimes I think she does like him. But Mary Edwards is rather prim and reserved; I do not always know what she would be at.'

'Unless Sam feels on sure ground with the lady herself, it seems a pity to me that he should be encouraged to think of her at all.'

'A young man must think of somebody,' said Elizabeth, 'and why should not he be as lucky as Robert, who has got a good wife and six thousand pounds?'

'We must not all expect to be individually lucky,' replied Emma. 'The luck of one member of a family is luck to all.'

'Mine is all to come, I am sure,' said Elizabeth, giving another sigh to the remembrance of Purvis. 'I have been unlucky enough, and I cannot say much for you, as my aunt married again so foolishly. Well – you will have a good ball, I dare say. The next turning will bring us to the turnpike. You may see the church tower over the hedge, and the White Hart is close by it. I shall long to know what you think of Tom Musgrave.'

## Chapter Two

SUCH WERE THE last audible sounds of Miss Watson's voice, before they passed through the turnpike gate and entered on the pitching of the town, the jumbling and noise of which made farther conversation most thoroughly undesirable. The old mare trotted heavily on, wanting no direction of the reins to take the right turning, and making only one blunder, in proposing to stop at the milliner's, before she drew up to Mr Edwards' door. Mr Edwards lived in the best house in the street, and the best in the place, if Mr Tomlinson the banker might be indulged in calling his newly erected house at the end of the town with a shrubbery and sweep in the country. Mr Edwards' house was higher than most of its neighbours with two windows on each side the door, the windows guarded by posts and chain, the door approached by a flight of stone steps.

'Here we are,' said Elizabeth, as the carriage ceased moving, 'safely arrived, and by the market clock we have been only five and thirty minutes coming, which *I* think is doing pretty well, though it would be nothing for Penelope. Is not it a nice town? The Edwardses have a noble house, you see, and they live quite in style. The door will be opened by a man in livery with a powdered head, I can tell you.'

Emma had seen the Edwardses only one morning at Stanton; they were therefore all but strangers to her, and though her spirits were by no means insensible to the expected joys of the evening, she felt a little uncomfortable in the thought of all that was to precede them. Her conversation with Elizabeth, too, giving her some very unpleasant feelings with respect to her own family, had made her more open to disagreeable impressions from any other cause, and increased her sense of the awkwardness of rushing into intimacy on so slight an acquaintance.

There was nothing in the manners of Mrs or Miss Edwards to give immediate change to these ideas; the mother, though a very friendly woman, had a reserved air and a great deal of formal civility, and the daughter, a genteel-looking girl of twenty-two with her hair in papers, seemed very naturally to have caught something of the style of the mother who had brought her up. Emma was soon left to know what they could be, by Elizabeth's being obliged to hurry away, and some very, very languid remarks on the probable brilliancy of the ball were all that broke at intervals a silence of half an hour before they were joined by the master of the house.

Mr Edwards had a much easier and more communicative air than the ladies of the family; he was fresh from the street, and he came ready to tell whatever might interest. After a cordial reception of Emma, he turned to his daughter with, 'Well, Mary, I bring you good news. The Osbornes will certainly be at the ball tonight. Horses for two carriages are ordered from the White Hart, to be at Osborne Castle by nine.'

'I am glad of it,' observed Mrs Edwards, 'because their coming gives a credit to our assemblies. The Osbornes being known to have been at the first ball will dispose a great many people to attend the second. It is more than they deserve, for in fact they add nothing to the pleasure of the evening, they come so late, and go so early, but great people have always their charm.'

Mr Edwards proceeded to relate every other little article of news which his morning's lounge had supplied him with, and they chatted with greater briskness, till Mrs Edwards' moment for dressing arrived, and the young ladies were carefully recommended to lose no time. Emma was shown to a very comfortable apartment, and as soon as Mrs Edwards' civilities could leave her to herself, the happy occupation, the first bliss of a ball began. The girls, dressing in some measure together, grew unavoidably better acquainted; Emma found in Miss Edwards the show of good sense, a modest unpretending mind, and a great wish of obliging, and when they returned to the parlour where Mrs Edwards was sitting, respectably attired in one of the two satin gowns which went through the winter, and a new cap from the milliner's, they entered it with much easier feelings and more natural smiles than they had taken away.

Their dress was now to be examined; Mrs Edwards acknowledged herself too old-fashioned to approve of every modern extravagance, however sanctioned, and though complacently viewing her daughter's good looks, would give but a qualified admiration; and Mr Edwards, not less satisfied with Mary, paid some compliments of good-humoured gallantry to Emma at her expense. The discussion led to more intimate remarks, and Miss Edwards gently asked Emma if she were not often reckoned very like her youngest brother. Emma thought she could perceive a faint blush accompany the question, and there seemed something still more suspicious in the manner in which Mr Edwards took up the subject.

'You are paying Miss Emma no great compliment, I think, Mary,' said he hastily. 'Mr Sam Watson is a very good sort of young man, and I dare say a very clever surgeon, but his complexion has been rather too much exposed to all weathers, to make a likeness to him very flattering.'

Mary apologised in some confusion. She had not thought a strong likeness at all incompatible with very different degrees of beauty. There might be a resemblance in countenance, and the complexion, and even the features, be very unlike.

'I know nothing of my brother's beauty,' said Emma, 'for I have not seen him since he was seven years old – but my father reckons us alike.'

'Mr Watson!' cried Mr Edwards. 'Well, you astonish me.

There is not the least likeness in the world; your brother's eyes are grey, yours are brown; he has a long face and a wide mouth. My dear, do *you* perceive the least resemblance?'

'Not the least. Miss Emma Watson puts me very much in mind of her eldest sister, and sometimes I see a look of Miss Penelope, and once or twice there has been a glance of Mr Robert, but I cannot perceive any likeness to Mr Samuel.'

'I see the likeness between her and Miss Watson,' replied Mr Edwards, 'very strongly, but I am not sensible of the others. I do not think she is like any of the family *but* Miss Watson, but I am very sure there is no resemblance between her and Sam.'

This matter was settled, and they went to dinner.

'Your father, Miss Emma, is one of my oldest friends,' said Mr Edwards, as he helped her to wine, when they were drawn round the fire to enjoy their dessert. 'We must drink to his better health. It is a great concern to me, I assure you, that he should be such an invalid. I know nobody who likes a game of cards in a social way better than he does, and very few people that play a fairer rubber. It is a thousand pities that he should be so deprived of the pleasure. For now we have a quiet little whist club that meets three times a week at the White Hart, and if he could but have his health, how much he would enjoy it!'

'I dare say he would, sir, and I wish with all my heart he were equal to it.'

'Your club would be better fitted for an invalid,' said Mrs Edwards, 'if you did not keep it up so late.'

This was an old grievance.

'So late, my dear, what are you talking of?' cried the husband with sturdy pleasantry. 'We are always at home before midnight. They would laugh at Osborne Castle to hear you call *that* late; they are but just rising from dinner at midnight.'

'That is nothing to the purpose,' retorted the lady calmly. 'The Osbornes are to be no rule for us. You had better meet every night, and break up two hours sooner.'

So far, the subject was very often carried, but Mr and Mrs Edwards were so wise as never to pass that point, and Mr Edwards now turned to something else. He had lived long enough in the idleness of a town to become a little of a gossip, and having some curiosity to know more of the circumstances of his young guest than had yet reached him, he began with:

'I think, Miss Emma, I remember your aunt very well about thirty years ago; I am pretty sure I danced with her in the old rooms at Bath, the year before I married. She was a very fine woman then, but like other people I suppose she is grown somewhat older since that time. I hope she is likely to be happy in her second choice.'

'I hope so, I believe so, sir,' said Emma in some agitation.

'Mr Turner had not been dead a great while, I think?'

'About two years, sir.'

'I forget what her name is now.'

'O'Brien.'

'Irish! Ah! I remember, and she is gone to settle in Ireland. I do not wonder that you should not wish to go with her into *that* country, Miss Emma, but it must be a great deprivation to her, poor lady! After bringing you up like a child of her own!'

'I was not so ungrateful, sir,' said Emma warmly, 'as to wish to be anywhere but with her. It did not suit them, it did not suit Captain O'Brien that I should be of the party.'

'Captain!' repeated Mrs Edwards. 'The gentleman is in the army, then?'

'Yes, ma'am.'

'Aye – there is nothing like your officers for captivating the ladies, young or old. There is no resisting a cockade, my dear.'

'I hope there is,' said Mrs Edwards gravely, with a quick glance at her daughter, and Emma had just recovered from her own perturbation in time to see a blush on Miss Edwards' cheek, and in remembering what Elizabeth had said of Captain Hunter, to wonder and waver between his influence and her brother's.

'Elderly ladies should be careful how they make a second choice,' observed Mr Edwards.

'Carefulness, discretion, should not be confined to elderly ladies, or to a second choice,' added his wife. 'It is quite as necessary to young ladies in their first.'

'Rather more so, my dear,' replied he, 'because young ladies are likely to feel the effects of it longer. When an old lady plays the fool, it is not in the course of nature that she should suffer from it many years.'

Emma drew her hand across her eyes, and Mrs Edwards on perceiving it changed the subject to one of less anxiety to all.

With nothing to do but expect the hour of setting off, the afternoon was long to the two young ladies, and though Miss Edwards was rather discomposed at the very early hour which her mother always fixed for going, that early hour itself was watched for with some eagerness. The entrance of the tea things at seven o'clock was some relief, and luckily Mr and Mrs Edwards always drank a dish extraordinary, and ate an additional muffin when they were going to sit up late, which lengthened the ceremony almost to the wished-for moment. At a little before eight, the Tomlinsons' carriage was heard to go by, which was the constant signal to Mrs Edwards to order hers to the door, and in a very few minutes, the party were transported from the quiet warmth of a snug parlour, to the bustle, noise and draughts of air of the broad entrance-passage of an inn.

Mrs Edwards, carefully guarding her own dress, while she attended with yet greater solicitude to the proper security of her young charges' shoulders and throats, led the way up the wide staircase, while no sound of a ball but the first scrape of one violin blessed the ears of her followers, and Miss Edwards, on hazarding the anxious enquiry of whether there were many people come yet, was told by the waiter as she knew she should, that 'Mr Tomlinson's family were in the room'. In passing along a short gallery to the Assembly Room, brilliant in lights before them, they were accosted by a young man in morning dress and boots, who was standing in the doorway of a bedchamber, apparently on purpose to see them go by.

'Ah! Mrs Edwards, how do you do? How do you do, Miss Edwards?' he cried, with an easy air. 'You are determined to be in good time, I see, as usual. The candles are but this moment lit.'

'I like to get a good seat by the fire, you know, Mr Musgrave,' replied Mrs Edwards.

'I am this moment going to dress,' said he. 'I am waiting for my stupid fellow. We shall have a famous ball; the Osbornes are certainly coming, you may depend upon *that*, for I was with Lord Osborne this morning.'

The party passed on. Mrs Edwards' satin gown swept along the clean floor of the ballroom to the fireplace at the upper end, where one party only were formally seated, while three or four officers were lounging together, passing in and out from the adjoining card-room. A very stiff meeting between these near neighbours ensued, and as soon as they were all duly placed again, Emma, in the low whisper which became the solemn scene, said to Miss Edwards:

'The gentleman we passed in the passage was Mr Musgrave, then? He is reckoned remarkably agreeable, I understand.'

Miss Edwards answered hesitatingly, 'Yes – he is very much liked by many people. But *we* are not very intimate.'

'He is rich, is not he?'

'He has about eight or nine hundred pounds a year, I believe. He came into possession of it when he was very young, and my father and mother think it has given him rather an unsettled turn. He is no favourite with them.'

The cold and empty appearance of the room and the demure air of the small cluster of females at one end of it began soon to give way; the inspiriting sound of other carriages was heard, and continual accessions of portly chaperons, and strings of smartly-dressed girls were received, with now and then a fresh gentleman straggler, who if not enough in love to station himself near any fair creature, seemed glad to escape into the card-room. Among the increasing numbers of military men, one now made his way to Miss Edwards, with an air of *empressement*, which decidedly said to her companion, 'I am Captain Hunter', and Emma, who could not but watch her at such a moment, saw her looking rather distressed, but by no means displeased, and heard an engagement formed for the two first dances, which made her think her brother Sam's a hopeless case.

Emma, in the meanwhile, was not unobserved or unadmired herself. A new face, and a very pretty one, could not be slighted; her name was whispered from one party to another, and no sooner had the signal been given by the orchestra's striking up a favourite air, which seemed to call the young men to their duty, and people the centre of the room, than she found herself engaged to dance with a brother officer, introduced by Captain Hunter. Emma Watson was not more than of the middle height, well-made and plump, with an air of healthy vigour. Her skin was very brown, but clear, smooth, and glowing, which with a lively eye, a sweet smile, and an open countenance, gave beauty to attract, and expression to make that beauty improve on acquaintance. Having no reason to be dissatisfied with her partner, the evening began very pleasantly to her, and her feelings perfectly coincided with the reiterated observation of others, that it was an excellent ball.

The first two dances were not quite over, when the returning sound of carriages after a long interruption called general notice, and 'the Osbornes are coming, the Osbornes are coming' was repeated round the room. After some minutes of extraordinary bustle without, and watchful curiosity within, the important party, preceded by the attentive master of the inn to open a door which was never shut, made their appearance. They consisted of Lady Osborne; her son Lord Osborne; her daughter Miss Osborne; Miss Carr, her daughter's friend; Mr Howard, formerly tutor to Lord Osborne, now clergyman of the parish in which the castle stood; Mrs Blake, a widow-sister who lived with him; her son, a fine boy of ten years old; and Mr Tom Musgrave, who probably, imprisoned within his own room, had been listening in bitter impatience to the sound of the music for the last half-hour. In their progress up the room, they paused almost immediately behind Emma, to receive the compliments of some acquaintance, and she heard Lady Osborne observe that they had made a point of coming early for the gratification of Mrs Blake's little boy, who was uncommonly fond of dancing. Emma looked at them all as they passed, but chiefly and with most interest on Tom Musgrave, who was certainly a genteel, good-looking young man. Of the females, Lady Osborne had by much the finest person; though nearly fifty, she was very handsome, and had all the dignity of rank.

Lord Osborne was a very fine young man, but there was an air of coldness, of carelessness, even of awkwardness about him, which seemed to speak him out of his element in a ballroom. He came in fact only because it was judged expedient for him to please the borough; he was not fond of women's company, and he never danced. Mr Howard was an agreeable-looking man, a little more than thirty.

At the conclusion of the two dances, Emma found herself, she knew not how, seated among the Osborne set, and she was immediately struck with the fine countenance and animated gestures of the little boy, as he was standing before his mother, wondering when they should begin.

'You will not be surprised at Charles's impatience,' said Mrs Blake, a lively, pleasant-looking little woman of five or six and thirty, to a lady who was standing near her, 'when you know what a partner he is to have. Miss Osborne has been so very kind as to promise to dance the two first dances with him.'

'Oh! yes – we have been engaged this week,' cried the boy, 'and we are to dance down every couple!'

On the other side of Emma, Miss Osborne, Miss Carr, and a party of young men were standing engaged in very lively consultation, and soon afterwards she saw the smartest officer of the set walking off to the orchestra to order the dance, while Miss Osborne, passing before her, to her little expecting partner hastily said, 'Charles, I beg your pardon for not keeping my engagement, but I am going to dance these two dances with Colonel Beresford. I know you will excuse me, and I will certainly dance with you after tea.'

And without staying for an answer, she turned again to Miss Carr, and in another minute was led by Colonel Beresford to begin the set. If the poor little boy's face had in its happiness been interesting to Emma, it was infinitely more so under this sudden reverse; he stood the picture of disappointment, with crimsoned cheeks, quivering lips, and eyes bent on the floor. His mother, stifling her own mortification, tried to soothe his, with the prospect of Miss Osborne's second promise, but though he contrived to utter with an effort of boyish bravery, 'Oh! I do not mind it', it was very evident by the unceasing agitation of his features that he minded it as much as ever. Emma did not think, or reflect; she felt and acted.

'I shall be very happy to dance with you, sir, if you like it,' said she, holding out her hand with the most unaffected good humour.

The boy, in one moment restored to all his first delight, looked joyfully at his mother and stepping forwards with an honest and simple, 'Thank you, ma'am', was instantly ready to attend his new acquaintance. The thankfulness of Mrs Blake was more diffuse; with a look, most expressive of unexpected pleasure and lively gratitude, she turned to her neighbour with repeated and fervent acknowledgements of so great and condescending a kindness to her boy. Emma with perfect truth could assure her that she could not be giving greater pleasure than she felt herself, and Charles being provided with his gloves and charged to keep them on, they joined the set which was now rapidly forming, with nearly equal complacency.

It was a partnership which could not be noticed without surprise. It gained her a broad stare from Miss Osborne and Miss Carr as they passed her in the dance.

'Upon my word, Charles, you are in luck,' (said the former as she turned him), 'you have got a better partner than me'; to which the happy Charles answered, 'Yes.'

Tom Musgrave, who was dancing with Miss Carr, gave her many inquisitive glances, and after a time Lord Osborne himself came and under pretence of talking to Charles stood to look at his partner. Though rather distressed by such observation, Emma could not repent what she had done, so happy had it made both the boy and his mother, the latter of whom was continually making opportunities of addressing her with the warmest civility. Her little partner she found, though bent chiefly on dancing, was not unwilling to speak when her questions or remarks gave him anything to say, and she learned, by a sort of inevitable enquiry, that he had two brothers and a sister, that they and their Mama all lived with his uncle at Wickstead, that his uncle taught him Latin, that he was very fond of riding, and had a horse of his own given him by Lord Osborne, and that he had been out once already with Lord Osborne's hounds.

At the end of these dances Emma found they were to drink tea; Miss Edwards gave her a caution to be at hand, in a manner which convinced her of Mrs Edwards' holding it very important to have them both close to her when she moved into the tea-room, and Emma was accordingly on the alert to gain her proper station. It was always the pleasure of the company to have a little bustle and crowd when they thus adjourned for refreshment. The tea-room was a small room within the card-room, and in passing through the latter, where the passage was straitened by tables, Mrs Edwards and her party were for a few moments hemmed in. It happened close by Lady Osborne's cassino table; Mr Howard who belonged to it spoke to his nephew; and Emma, on perceiving herself the object of attention both to Lady Osborne and him, had just turned away her eyes in time to avoid seeming to hear her young companion delightedly whisper aloud, 'Oh! Uncle, do look at my partner. She is so pretty!' As they were immediately in motion again, however, Charles was hurried off without being able to receive his uncle's suffrage.

On entering the tea-room, in which two long tables were prepared, Lord Osborne was to be seen quite alone at the end of one, as if retreating as far as he could from the ball, to enjoy his own thoughts and gape without restraint. Charles instantly pointed him out to Emma.

'There's Lord Osborne. Let you and I go sit by him.'

'No, no,' said Emma, laughing, 'you must sit with my friends.'

Charles was now free enough to hazard a few questions in his turn.

'What o'clock was it?'

'Eleven.'

'Eleven! And I am not at all sleepy. Mama said I should be asleep before ten. Do you think Miss Osborne will keep her word with me, when tea is over?'

'Oh, yes, I suppose so' – though she felt that she had no better reason to give than that Miss Osborne had *not* kept it before.

'When shall you come to Osborne Castle?'

'Never, probably. I am not acquainted with the family.'

'But you may come to Wickstead and see Mama, and she can take you to the Castle. There is a monstrous curious stuffed fox there, and a badger – anybody would think they were alive. It is a pity you should not see them.'

On rising from tea, there was again a scramble for the pleasure of being first out of the room, which happened to be increased by one or two of the card parties having just broken up and the players being disposed to move exactly the different way. Among these was Mr Howard, his sister leaning on his arm, and no sooner were they within reach of Emma, than Mrs Blake calling her notice by a friendly touch, said, 'Your goodness to Charles, my dear Miss Watson, brings all his family upon you. Give me leave to introduce my brother, Mr Howard.'

Emma curtsied, the gentleman bowed – made a hasty request for the honour of her hand in the next two dances, to which as hasty an affirmative was given, and they were immediately impelled in opposite directions. Emma was very well pleased with the circumstance; there was a quietly- cheerful, gentlemanlike air in Mr Howard which suited her, and in a few minutes afterwards, the value of her engagement increased, when as she was sitting in the card-room somewhat screened by a door, she heard Lord Osborne, who was lounging on a vacant table near her, call Tom Musgrave towards him and say, 'Why do you not dance with that beautiful Emma Watson? I want you to dance with her, and I will come and stand by you.'

'I was determining on it this very moment, my lord; I'll be introduced and dance with her directly'

'Aye, do – and if you find she does not want much talking to, you may introduce me by and by.'

'Very well, my lord. If she is like her sisters, she will only want to be listened to. I will go this moment. I shall find her in the tea-room. That stiff old Mrs Edwards has never done tea.'

Away he went, Lord Osborne after him, and Emma lost no time in hurrying from her corner, exactly the other way, forgetting in her haste that she left Mrs Edwards behind.

'We had quite lost you,' said Mrs Edwards, who followed her with Mary, in less than five minutes. 'If you prefer this room to the other, there is no reason why you should not be here, but we had better all be together.'

Emma was saved the trouble of apologising by their being joined at the moment by Tom Musgrave, who requesting Mrs Edwards aloud to do him the honour of presenting him to Miss Emma Watson, left that good lady without any choice in the business, but that of testifying by the coldness of her manner that she did it unwillingly. The honour of dancing with her was solicited without loss of time, and Emma, however she might like to be thought a beautiful girl by lord or commoner, was so little disposed to favour Tom Musgrave himself, that she had considerable satisfaction in avowing her prior engagement.

He was evidently surprised and discomposed. The style of her last partner had probably led him to believe her not over-powered with applications.

'My little friend Charles Blake,' he cried, 'must not expect to engross you the whole evening! We can never suffer this. It is against the rules of the assembly, and I am sure it will never be patronised by our good friend here, Mrs Edwards; she is by much too nice a judge of decorum to give her licence to such a dangerous particularity.'

'I am not going to dance with Master Blake, sir.'

The gentleman, a little disconcerted, could only hope he might be more fortunate another time, and seeming unwilling to leave her, though his friend Lord Osborne was waiting in the doorway for the result, as Emma with some amusement perceived, he began to make civil enquiries after her family.

'How comes it that we have not the pleasure of seeing your sisters here this evening? Our assemblies have been used to be so well treated by them, that we do not know how to take this neglect.'

'My eldest sister is the only one at home, and she could not leave my father.'

'Miss Watson the only one at home! You astonish me! It seems but the day before yesterday that I saw them all three in this town. But I am afraid I have been a very sad neighbour of late. I hear dreadful complaints of my negligence wherever I go, and I confess it is a shameful length of time since I was at Stanton. But I shall *now* endeavour to make myself amends for the past.'

Emma's calm curtsey in reply must have struck him as very unlike the encouraging warmth he had been used to receive from her sisters, and gave him probably the novel sensation of doubting his own influence, and of wishing for more attention than she bestowed. The dancing now recommenced; Miss Carr being impatient to *call*, everybody was required to stand up, and Tom Musgrave's curiosity was appeased on seeing Mr Howard come forward and claim Emma's hand. 'That will do as well for me,' was Lord Osborne's remark, when his friend carried him the news, and he was continually at Howard's elbow during the two dances. The frequency of his appearance there was the only unpleasant part of her engagement, the only objection she could make to Mr Howard. In himself, she thought him as agreeable as he looked; though chatting on the commonest topics he had a sensible, unaffected way of expressing himself which made them all worth hearing, and she only regretted that he had not been able to make his pupil's manners as unexceptionable as his own.

The two dances seemed very short, and she had her partner's authority for considering them so. At their conclusion the Osbornes and their train were all on the move.

'We are off at last,' said his lordship to Tom. 'How much longer do *you* stay in this heavenly place? – till sunrise?'

'No, faith! my lord, I have had quite enough of it. I assure you, I shall not show myself here again when I have had the honour of attending Lady Osborne to her carriage. I shall retreat in as much secrecy as possible to the most remote corner of the house, where I shall order a barrel of oysters, and be famously snug.'

'Let us see you soon at the Castle, and bring me word how she looks by daylight.'

Emma and Mrs Blake parted as old acquaintance, and Charles shook her by the hand and wished her 'goodbye' at least a dozen times. From Miss Osborne and Miss Carr she received something like a jerking curtsey as they passed her; even Lady Osborne gave her a look of complacency, and his lordship actually came back after the others were out of the room, to 'beg her pardon', and look in the window seat behind her for the gloves which were visibly compressed in his hand.

As Tom Musgrave was seen no more, we may suppose his plan to have succeeded, and imagine him mortifying with his barrel of oysters, in dreary solitude, or gladly assisting the landlady in her bar to make fresh negus for the happy dancers above. Emma could not help missing the party by whom she had been, though in some respects unpleasantly, distinguished, and the two dances which followed and concluded the ball were rather flat, in comparison with the others. Mr Edwards having played with good luck, they were some of the last in the room.

## Chapter Three

'HERE WE ARE, back again, I declare,' said Emma sorrowfully, as she walked into the dining-room, where the table was prepared, and the neat upper maid was lighting the candles. 'My dear Miss Edwards, how soon it is at an end! I wish it could all come over again!'

A great deal of kind pleasure was expressed in her having enjoyed the evening so much, and Mr Edwards was as warm as herself in praise of the fullness, brilliancy and spirit of the meeting, though as he had been fixed the whole time at the same table in the same room, with only one change of chairs, it might have seemed a matter scarcely perceived. But he had won four rubbers out of five, and everything went well. His daughter felt the advantage of his gratified state of mind, in the course of the remarks and retrospections which now ensued, over the welcome soup.

'How came you not to dance with either of the Mr Tomlinsons, Mary?' said her mother.

'I was always engaged when they asked me.'

'I thought you were to have stood up with Mr James, the last two dances; Mrs Tomlinson told me he was gone to ask you – and I had heard you say two minutes before that you were *not* engaged.'

'Yes, but – there was a mistake – I had misunderstood – I did not know I was engaged. I thought it had been for the two dances after, if we stayed so long, but Captain Hunter assured me it was for those very two.'

'So you ended with Captain Hunter, Mary, did you?' said her father. 'And who did you begin with?'

'Captain Hunter,' was repeated, in a very humble tone.

'Hum! That is being constant however. But who else did you dance with?'

'Mr Norton, and Mr Styles.'

'And who are they?'

'Mr Norton is a cousin of Captain Hunter's.'

'And who is Mr Styles?'

'One of his particular friends.'

'All in the same regiment,' added Mrs Edwards. 'Mary was surrounded by red coats the whole evening. I should have been better pleased to see her dancing with some of our old neighbours, I confess.'

'Yes, yes, we must not neglect our old neighbours. But if these soldiers are quicker than other people in a ballroom, what are young ladies to do?'

'I think there is no occasion for their engaging themselves so many dances beforehand, Mr Edwards.'

'No, perhaps not, but I remember, my dear, when you and I did the same.'

Mrs Edwards said no more, and Mary breathed again. A great deal of good-humoured pleasantry followed, and Emma went to bed in charming spirits, her head full of Osbornes, Blakes and Howards.

The next morning brought a great many visitors. It was the way of the place always to call on Mrs Edwards on the morning after a ball, and this neighbourly inclination was increased in the present instance by a general spirit of curiosity on Emma's account, as everybody wanted to look again at the girl who had been admired the night before by Lord Osborne.

Many were the eyes, and various the degrees of approbation with which she was examined. Some saw no fault, and some no beauty. With some her brown skin was the annihilation of every grace, and others could never be persuaded that she were half so handsome as Elizabeth Watson had been ten years ago. The morning passed quietly away in discussing the merits of the ball with all this succession of company, and Emma was at once astonished by finding it two o'clock, and considering that she had heard nothing of her father's chair. After this discovery she had walked twice to the window to examine the street, and was on the point of asking leave to ring the bell and make enquiries, when the light sound of a carriage driving up to the door set her heart at ease. She stepped again to the window, but instead of the convenient but very un-smart family equipage perceived a neat curricle. Mr Musgrave was shortly afterwards announced, and Mrs Edwards put on her very stiffest look at the sound. Not at all dismayed however by her chilling air, he paid his compliments to each of the ladies with no unbecoming ease, and continuing to address Emma, presented her a note, which he had the honour of bringing her from her sister; but to which he must observe that a verbal postscript from himself would be requisite.

The note, which Emma was beginning to read rather *before* Mrs Edwards had entreated her to use no ceremony, contained a few lines from Elizabeth importing that their father in consequence of being unusually well had taken the sudden resolution of attending the visitation that day, and that as his road lay quite wide from R., it was impossible for her to come home till the following morning, unless the Edwardses would send her, which was hardly to be expected, or she could meet with any chance conveyance, or did not mind walking so far.

She had scarcely run her eye through the whole, before she found herself obliged to listen to Tom Musgrave's farther account. 'I received that note from the fair hands of Miss Watson only ten minutes ago,' said he; 'I met her in the village of Stanton, whither my good stars prompted me to turn my horses' heads; she was at that moment in quest of a person to employ on the errand, and I was fortunate enough to convince her that she could not find a more willing or speedy messenger than myself. Remember, I say nothing of my disinterestedness. My reward is to be the indulgence of conveying you to Stanton in my curricle. Though they are not written down, I bring your sister's orders for the same.'

Emma felt distressed; she did not like the proposal; she did not wish to be on terms of intimacy with the proposer, and yet fearful of encroaching on the Edwardses, as well as wishing to go home herself, she was at a loss how entirely to decline what he offered. Mrs Edwards continued silent, either not understanding the case, or waiting to see how the young lady's inclination lay. Emma thanked him, but professed herself very unwilling to give him so much trouble. The trouble was, of course, honour, pleasure, delight. What had he or his horses to do? Still she hesitated. She believed she must beg leave to decline his assistance – she was rather afraid of the sort of carriage. The distance was not beyond a walk. Mrs Edwards was silent no longer. She enquired into the particulars, and then said:

'We shall be extremely happy, Miss Emma, if you can give us the pleasure of your company till tomorrow, but if you cannot conveniently do so, our carriage is quite at your service, and Mary will be pleased with the opportunity of seeing your sister.'

This was precisely what Emma had longed for, and she accepted the offer most thankfully, acknowledging that as Elizabeth was entirely alone, it was her wish to return home to dinner. The plan was warmly opposed by their visitor.

'I cannot suffer it, indeed. I must not be deprived of the happiness of escorting you. I assure you there is not a possibility of fear with my horses. You might guide them yourself. *Your sisters* all know how quiet they are; they have none of them the smallest scruple in trusting themselves with me, even on a race course. Believe me,' added he, lowering his voice, '*you* are quite safe, the danger is only *mine*.'

Emma was not more disposed to oblige him for all this.

'And as to Mrs Edwards' carriage being used the day after a ball, it is a thing quite out of rule, I assure you – never heard of before – the old coachman will look as black as his horses. Won't he, Miss Edwards?'

No notice was taken. The ladies were silently firm, and the gentleman found himself obliged to submit.

'What a famous ball we had last night!' he cried, after a short pause. 'How long did you keep it up, after the Osbornes and I went away?'

'We had two dances more.'

'It is making it too much of a fatigue, I think, to stay so late. I suppose your set was not a very full one.'

'Yes, quite as full as ever, except the Osbornes. There seemed no vacancy anywhere, and everybody danced with uncommon spirit to the very last.'

Emma said this, though against her conscience.

'Indeed! perhaps I might have looked in upon you again, if I had been aware of as much, for I am rather fond of dancing than not. Miss Osborne is a charming girl, is not she?'

'I do not think her handsome,' replied Emma, to whom all this was chiefly addressed.

'Perhaps she is not critically handsome, but her manners are delightful. And Fanny Carr is a most interesting little creature. You can imagine nothing more *naive* or *piquante*. And what do you think of *Lord* Osborne, Miss Watson?'

'That he would be handsome, even though he were *not* a lord – and perhaps – better bred, more desirous of pleasing, and showing himself pleased in a right place.'

'Upon my word, you are severe upon my friend! I assure you Lord Osborne is a very good fellow.'

'I do not dispute his virtues – but I do not like his careless air.'

'If it were not a breach of confidence,' replied Tom with an important look, 'perhaps I might be able to win a more favour-able opinion of poor Osborne.'

Emma gave him no encouragement, and he was obliged to keep his friend's secret. He was also obliged to put an end to his visit, for Mrs Edwards having ordered her carriage, there was no time to be lost on Emma's side in preparing for it. Miss Edwards accompanied her home, but as it was dinner hour at Stanton, stayed with them only a few minutes.

'Now, my dear Emma,' said Miss Watson, as soon as they were alone, 'you must talk to me all the rest of the day, without stopping, or I shall not be satisfied. But first of all Nanny shall bring in the dinner. Poor thing! You will not dine as you did yesterday, for we have nothing except some fried beef. How nice Mary Edwards looks in her new pelisse! And now tell me how you like them all, and what I am to say to Sam. I have begun my letter, Jack Stokes is to call for it tomorrow, for his uncle is going within a mile of Guildford the next day.'

Nanny brought in the dinner. 'We will wait upon ourselves,' continued Elizabeth, 'then we shall lose no time. And so, you would not come home with Tom Musgrave?'

'No. You had said so much against him that I could not wish either for the obligation, or the intimacy which the use of his carriage must have created. I should not even have liked the appearance of it.'

'You did very right, though I wonder at your forbearance, and I do not think I could have done it myself. He seemed so eager to fetch you that I could not say no, though it rather went against me to be throwing you together, so well as I knew his tricks, but I did long to see you, and it was a clever way of getting you home; besides, it won't do to be too nice. Nobody could have thought of the Edwardses letting you have their coach, after the horses being out so late. But what am I to say to Sam?'

'If you are guided by me, you will not encourage him to think of Miss Edwards. The father is decidedly against him, the mother shows him no favour, and I doubt his having any interest with Mary. She danced twice with Captain Hunter, and I think shows him in general as much encouragement as is consistent with her disposition and the circumstances she is placed in. She once mentioned Sam, and certainly with a little confusion, but that was perhaps merely owing to the consciousness of his liking her, which may very probably have come to her knowledge.'

'Oh, dear, yes! she has heard enough of that from us all. Poor Sam! He is out of luck as well as other people. For the life of me, Emma, I cannot help feeling for those that are crossed in love. Well, now begin, and give me an account of everything as it happened.'

Emma obeyed her, and Elizabeth listened with very little interruption till she heard of Mr Howard as a partner.

'Dance with Mr Howard – good heavens! You don't say so! Why, he is quite one of the great and grand ones. Did not you find him very high?'

'His manners are of a kind to give *me* much more ease and confidence than Tom Musgrave's.'

'Well, go on. I should have been frightened out of my wits, to have had anything to do with the Osbornes' set.'

Emma concluded her narration.

'And so you really did not dance with Tom Musgrave at all? But you must have liked him, you must have been struck with him altogether.'

'I do *not* like him, Elizabeth. I allow his person and air to be good, and that his manners to a certain point – his address rather – is pleasing. But I see nothing else to admire in him. On the contrary, he seems very vain, very conceited, absurdly anxious for distinction, and absolutely contemptible in some of the measures he takes for becoming so. There is a ridiculousness about him that entertains me, but his company gives me no other agreeable emotion.'

'My dearest Emma! You are like nobody else in the world. It is well Margaret is not by. You do not offend *me,* though I hardly know how to believe you. But Margaret would never forgive such words.'

'I wish Margaret could have heard him profess his ignorance of her being out of the country; he declared it seemed only two days since he had seen her.'

'Aye, that is just like him, and yet this is the man she *will* fancy so desperately in love with her. He is no favourite of mine, as you well know, Emma, but you must think him agreeable. Can you lay your hand on your heart, and say you do not?'

'Indeed I can, both hands, and spread to their widest extent.'

'I should like to know the man you *do* think agreeable.'

'His name is Howard.'

'Howard! Dear me, I cannot think of *him,* but as playing cards with Lady Osborne, and looking proud. I must own, however, that it is a relief to me to find you can speak as you do of Tom Musgrave; my heart did misgive me that you would like him too well. You talked so stoutly beforehand that I was sadly afraid your brag would be punished. I only hope it will last, and that he will not come on to pay you much attention; it is a hard thing for a woman to stand against the flattering ways of a man, when he is bent upon pleasing her.'

As their quietly-sociable little meal concluded, Miss Watson could not help observing how comfortably it had passed. 'It is so delightful to me,' said she, 'to have things going on in peace and good humour. Nobody can tell how much I hate quarrelling. Now, though we have had nothing but fried beef, how good it has all seemed. I wish everybody were as easily satisfied as you, but poor Margaret is very snappish, and Penelope owns she had rather have quarrelling going on, than nothing at all.'

Mr Watson returned in the evening, not the worse for the

exertion of the day, and consequently pleased with what he had done, and glad to talk of it over his own fireside. Emma had not foreseen any interest to herself in the occurrences of a visitation, but when she heard Mr Howard spoken of as the preacher, and as having given them an excellent sermon, she could not help listening with a quicker ear.

'I do not know when I have heard a discourse more to my mind,' continued Mr Watson, 'or one better delivered. He reads extremely well, with great propriety and in a very impressive manner, and at the same time without any theatrical grimace or violence. I own, I do not like much action in the pulpit – I do not like the studied air and artificial inflections of voice which your very popular and most admired preachers generally have. A simple delivery is much better calculated to inspire devotion, and shows a much better taste. Mr Howard read like a scholar and a gentleman.'

'And what had you for dinner, sir?' said his eldest daughter.

He related the dishes and told what he had ate himself. 'Upon the whole,' he added, 'I have had a very comfortable day; my old friends were quite surprised to see me amongst them, and I must say that everybody paid me great attention, and seemed to feel for me as an invalid. They would make me sit near the fire, and as the partridges were pretty high, Dr Richards would have them sent away to the other end of the table, that they might not offend Mr Watson – which I thought very kind of him. But what pleased me as much as anything was Mr Howard's attention. There is a pretty steep flight of steps up to the room we dine in, which do not quite agree with my gouty foot, and Mr Howard walked by me from the bottom to the top, and would make me take his arm. It struck me as very becoming in so young a man, but I am sure I had no claim to expect it, for I never saw him before in my life. By and by, he enquired after one of my daughters, but I do not know which. I suppose you know among yourselves.'

## Chapter Four

ON THE THIRD day after the ball, as Nanny at five minutes before three was beginning to bustle into the parlour with the tray and the knife-case, she was suddenly called to the front door by the sound of as smart a rap as the end of a riding-whip could give, and though charged by Miss Watson to let nobody in, returned in half a minute, with a look of awkward dismay, to hold the parlour door open for Lord Osborne and Tom Musgrave.

The surprise of the young ladies may be imagined. No visitors would have been welcome at such a moment, but such visitors as these – such a one as Lord Osborne at least, a nobleman and a stranger – was really distressing. He looked a little embarrassed himself, as, on being introduced by his easy, voluble friend, he muttered something of doing himself the honour of waiting on Mr Watson. Though Emma could not but take the compliment of the visit to herself, she was very far from enjoying it. She felt all the inconsistency of such an acquaintance with the very humble style in which they were obliged to live, and having in her aunt's family been used to many of the elegancies of life, was fully sensible of all that must be open to the ridicule of richer people in her present home.

Of the pain of such feelings Elizabeth knew very little; her simpler mind or juster reason saved her from such mortification, and though shrinking under a general sense of inferiority, she felt no particular shame. Mr Watson, as the gentlemen had already heard from Nanny, was not well enough to be downstairs. With much concern they took their seats, Lord Osborne near Emma, and the convenient Mr Musgrave in high spirits at his own importance, on the other side of the fireplace with Elizabeth. *He* was at no loss for words, but when Lord Osborne had hoped that Emma had not caught cold at the ball, he had nothing more to say for some time, and could only gratify his eye by occasional glances at his fair neighbour.

Emma was not inclined to give herself much trouble for his entertainment, and after hard labour of mind, he produced the remark of its being a very fine day, and followed it up with the question of, 'Have you been walking this morning?'

'No, my lord. We thought it too dirty.'

'You should wear half-boots.' After another pause, 'Nothing sets off a neat ankle more than a half-boot; nankin galoshed with black looks very well. Do not you like half-boots?'

'Yes, but unless they are so stout as to injure their beauty, they are not fit for country walking.'

'Ladies should ride in dirty weather. Do you ride?'

'No, my lord.'

'I wonder every lady does not. A woman never looks better than on horseback.'

'But every woman may not have the inclination, or the means.'

'If they knew how much it became them, they would all have the inclination, and I fancy, Miss Watson, when once they had the inclination, the means would soon follow.'

'Your lordship thinks we always have our own way. *That* is a point on which ladies and gentlemen have long disagreed. But without pretending to decide it, I may say that there are some circumstances which even *women* cannot control. Female economy will do a great deal, my lord, but it cannot turn a small income into a large one.'

Lord Osborne was silenced. Her manner had been neither sententious nor sarcastic, but there was a something in its mild seriousness, as well as in the words themselves, which made his lordship think, and when he addressed again, it was with a degree of considerate propriety, totally unlike the half-awkward, half-fearless style of his former remarks. It was a new thing with him to wish to please a woman; it was the first time that he had ever felt what was due to a woman in Emma's situation. But as he wanted neither sense nor a good disposition, he did not feel it without effect.

'You have not been long in this country, I understand,' said he in the tone of a gentleman. 'I hope you are pleased with it.'

He was rewarded by a gracious answer, and a more liberal full view of her face than she had yet bestowed. Unused to exert himself, and happy in contemplating her, he then sat in silence for some minutes longer, while Tom Musgrave was chattering to Elizabeth, till they were interrupted by Nanny's approach, who half opening the door and putting in her head, said:

'Please ma'am, Master wants to know why he ben't to have his dinner.'

The gentlemen, who had hitherto disregarded every symptom, however positive, of the nearness of that meal, now jumped up with apologies, while Elizabeth briskly called after Nanny 'to tell Betty to take up the fowls'.

'I am sorry it happens so,' she added, turning good-humouredly towards Musgrave, 'but you know what early hours we keep.'

Tom had nothing to say for himself; he knew it very well, and such honest simplicity, such shameless truth, rather bewildered him. Lord Osborne's parting compliments took some time, his inclination for speech seeming to increase with the shortness of the term for indulgence. He recommended exercise in defiance of dirt, spoke again in praise of half-boots, begged that his sister might be allowed to send Emma the name of her shoemaker, and concluded with saying, 'My hounds will be hunting this country next week – I believe they will throw off at

Stanton Wood on Wednesday at nine o'clock. I mention this, in hopes of your being drawn out to see what's going on. If the morning's tolerable, pray do us the honour of giving us your good wishes in person.'

The sisters looked on each other with astonishment, when their visitors had withdrawn.

'Here's an unaccountable honour!' cried Elizabeth at last. 'Who would have thought of Lord Osborne's coming to Stanton? He is very handsome, but Tom Musgrave looks all to nothing, the smartest and most fashionable man of the two. I am glad he did not say anything to me; I would not have had to talk to such a great man for the world. Tom was very agreeable, was not he? But did you hear him ask where Miss Penelope and Miss Margaret were, when he first came in? It put me out of patience. I am glad Nanny had not laid the cloth, however, it would have looked so awkward; just the tray did not signify.'

To say that Emma was not flattered by Lord Osborne's visit would be to assert a very unlikely thing, and describe a very odd young lady, but the gratification was by no means unalloyed; his coming was a sort of notice which might please her vanity, but did not suit her pride, and she would rather have known that he wished the visit without presuming to make it than have seen him at Stanton. Among other unsatisfactory feelings it once occurred to her to wonder why Mr Howard had not taken the same privilege of coming, and accompanied his lordship, but she was willing to suppose that he had either known nothing about it, or had declined any share in a measure which carried quite as much impertinence in its form as good breeding.

Mr Watson was very far from being delighted when he heard what had passed; a little peevish under immediate pain, and ill-disposed to be pleased, he only replied, 'Phoo, phoo! what occasion could there be for Lord Osborne's coming? I have lived here fourteen years without being noticed by any of the family. It is some foolery of that idle fellow Tom Musgrave. I cannot return the visit. I would not if I could.' And when Tom Musgrave was met with again, he was commissioned with a message of excuse to Osborne Castle, on the too-sufficient plea of Mr Watson's infirm state of health.

A week or ten days rolled quietly away after this visit before any new bustle arose to interrupt, even for half a day, the tranquil and affectionate intercourse of the two sisters, whose mutual regard was increasing with the intimate knowledge of each other which such intercourse produced. The first circumstance to break in on this serenity was the receipt of a letter from Croydon to announce the speedy return of Margaret, and a visit of two or three days from Mr and Mrs Robert Watson, who undertook to bring her home and wished to see their sister Emma.

It was an expectation to fill the thoughts of the sisters at Stanton, and to busy the hours of one of them at least, for as Jane had been a woman of fortune, the preparations for her entertainment were considerable, and as Elizabeth had at all times more goodwill than method in her guidance of the house, she could make no change without a bustle.

An absence of fourteen years had made all her brothers and sisters strangers to Emma, but in her expectation of Margaret there was more than the awkwardness of such an alienation; she had heard things which made her dread her return, and the day which brought the party to Stanton seemed to her the probable conclusion of almost all that had been comfortable in the house.

Robert Watson was an attorney at Croydon, in a good way of business, very well satisfied with himself for the same, and for having married the only daughter of the attorney to whom he had been clerk, with a fortune of six thousand pounds. Mrs Robert was not less pleased with herself for having had that six thousand pounds, and for being now in possession of a very smart house in Croydon, where she gave genteel parties, and wore fine clothes. In her person there was nothing remarkable; her manners were pert and conceited. Margaret was not without beauty; she had a slight, pretty figure, and rather wanted countenance than good features, but the sharp and anxious expression of her face made her beauty in general little felt. On meeting her long-absent sister, as on every occasion of show, her manner was all affection and her voice all gentleness; continual smiles and a very slow articulation being her constant resort when determined on pleasing.

She was now so 'delighted to see dear, dear Emma' that she could hardly speak a word in a minute. 'I am sure we shall be great friends,' she observed, with much sentiment, as they were sitting together. Emma scarcely knew how to answer such a proposition, and the manner in which it was spoken she could not attempt to equal. Mrs Robert Watson eyed her with much familiar curiosity and triumphant compassion; the loss of the aunt's fortune was uppermost in her mind at the moment of meeting, and she could not but feel how much better it was to be the daughter of a gentleman of property in Croydon, than the niece of an old woman who threw herself away on an Irish captain.

Robert was carelessly kind, as became a prosperous man and a brother; more intent on settling with the post-boy, inveighing against the exorbitant advance in posting, and pondering over a doubtful half-crown, than on welcoming a sister who was no longer likely to have any property for him to get the direction of.

'Your road through the village is infamous, Elizabeth,' said he, 'worse than ever it was. By heaven! I would indite it if I lived near you. Who is surveyor now?'

There was a little niece at Croydon, to be fondly enquired after by the kind-hearted Elizabeth, who regretted very much her not being of the party.

'You are very good,' replied her mother, 'and I assure you it went very hard with Augusta to have us come away without her. I was forced to say we were only going to church and promise to come back for her directly. But you know it would not do to bring her without her maid, and I am as particular as ever in having her properly attended to.'

'Sweet little darling!' cried Margaret. 'It quite broke my heart to leave her'

'Then why was you in such a hurry to run away from her?' cried Mrs Robert. 'You are a sad shabby girl. I have been quarrelling with you all the way we came, have not I? Such a visit as this I never heard of! You know how glad we are to have any of you with us, if it be for months together. And I am sorry' (with a witty smile) 'we have not been able to make Croydon agreeable this autumn.'

'My dearest Jane, do not overpower me with your raillery. You know what inducements I had to bring me home. Spare me, I entreat you; I am no match for your arch sallies.'

'Well, I only beg you will not set your neighbours against the place. Perhaps Emma may be tempted to go back with us, and stay till Christmas, if you don't put in your word.'

Emma was greatly obliged.

'I assure you we have very good society at Croydon. I do not much attend the balls, they are rather too mixed, but our parties are very select and good. I had seven tables last week in my drawing-room. Are you fond of the country? How do you like Stanton?'

'Very much,' replied Emma, who thought a comprehensive answer most to the purpose. She saw that her sister-in-law despised her immediately. Mrs Robert Watson was indeed wondering what sort of a home Emma could possibly have been used to in Shropshire, and setting it down as certain that her aunt could never have had six thousand pounds.

'How charming Emma is!' whispered Margaret to Mrs Robert in her most languishing tone. Emma was quite distressed by such behaviour, and she did not like it better when she heard Margaret five minutes afterwards say to Elizabeth in a sharp, quick accent, totally unlike the first:

'Have you heard from Penelope since she went to Chichester? I had a letter the other day. I don't find she is likely to make anything of it. I fancy she'll come back "Miss Penelope" as she went.'

Such, she feared, would be Margaret's common voice, when the novelty of her own appearance were over; the tone of artificial sensibility was not recommended by the idea. The ladies were invited upstairs to prepare for dinner.

'I hope you will find things tolerably comfortable, Jane,' said Elizabeth as she opened the door of the spare bedchamber.

'My good creature,' replied Jane, 'use no ceremony with me, I entreat you. I am one of those who always take things as they find them. I hope I can put up with a small apartment for two or three nights without making a piece of work. I always wish to be treated quite *en famille* when I come to see you, and now I do hope you have not been getting a great dinner for us. Remember we never eat suppers.'

'I suppose,' said Margaret rather quickly to Emma, 'you and I are to be together; Elizabeth always takes care to have a room to herself.'

'No, Elizabeth gives me half hers.'

'Oh' (in a softened voice, and rather mortified to find she was not ill-used), 'I am sorry I am not to have the pleasure of your company, especially as it makes me nervous to be much alone.'

Emma was the first of the females in the parlour again; on entering it she found her brother alone.

'So, Emma,' said he, 'you are quite the stranger at home. It must seem odd enough to you to be here. A pretty piece of work your Aunt Turner has made of it! By heaven! a woman should never be trusted with money. I always said she ought to have settled something on you, as soon as her husband died.'

'But that would have been trusting *me* with money,' replied Emma, 'and *I* am a woman too.'

'It might have been secured to your future use, without your having any power over it now. What a blow it must have been upon you! To find yourself, instead of heiress of eight or nine thousand pounds, sent back a weight upon your family, without a sixpence. I hope the old woman will smart for it.'

'Do not speak disrespectfully of her. She was very good to me, and if she has made an imprudent choice, she will suffer more from it herself, than *I* can possibly do.'

'I do not mean to distress you, but you know everybody must think her an old fool. I thought Turner had been reckoned an extraordinary sensible, clever man. How the devil came he to make such a will?'

'My uncle's sense is not at all impeached, in my opinion, by his attachment to my aunt. She had been an excellent wife to him. The most liberal and enlightened minds are always the most confiding. The event has been unfortunate, but my uncle's memory is, if possible, endeared to me by such a proof of tender respect for my aunt.'

'That's odd sort of talking! He might have provided decently for his widow, without leaving everything that he had to dispose of, or any part of it, at her mercy.'

'My aunt may have erred,' said Emma warmly, 'she *has* erred – but my uncle's conduct was faultless. I was her own niece, and he left to herself the power and the pleasure of providing for me.'

'But unluckily she has left the pleasure of providing for you to your father, and without the power. That's the long and short of the business. After keeping you at a distance from your family for such a length of time as must do away all natural affection among us, and breeding you up (I suppose) in a superior style, you are returned upon their hands without a sixpence.'

'You know,' replied Emma, struggling with her tears, 'my uncle's melancholy state of health. He was a greater invalid than my father. He could not leave home.'

'I do not mean to make you cry,' said Robert, rather softened, and after a short silence, by way of changing the subject, he added, 'I am just come from my father's room; he seems very indifferent. It will be a sad break-up when he dies. Pity you can none of you get married! You must come to Croydon as well as the rest, and see what you can do there. I believe if Margaret had had a thousand or fifteen hundred pounds, there was a young man who would have thought of her.'

Emma was glad when they were joined by the others; it was better to look at her sister-in-law's finery than listen to Robert, who had equally irritated and grieved her. Mrs Robert, exactly as smart as she had been at her own party, came in with apologies for her dress. 'I would not make you wait,' said she, 'so I put on the first thing I met with. I am afraid I am a sad figure. My dear Mr Watson' (to her husband) 'you have not put any fresh powder in your hair.'

'No – I do not intend it. I think there is powder enough in my hair for my wife and sisters.'

'Indeed, you ought to make some alteration in your dress before dinner when you are out visiting, though you do not at home.'

'Nonsense.'

'It is very odd you should not like to do what other gentlemen do. Mr Marshall and Mr Hemmings change their dress every day of their lives before dinner. And what was the use of my putting up your last new coat, if you are never to wear it?'

'Do be satisfied with being fine yourself, and leave your husband alone.'

To put an end to this altercation, and soften the evident vexation of her sister-in-law, Emma (though in no spirits to make such nonsense easy) began to admire her gown. It produced immediate complacency.

'Do you like it?' said she. 'I am very happy. It has been excessively admired, but sometimes I think the pattern too large. I shall wear one tomorrow that I think you will prefer to this. Have you seen the one I gave Margaret?'

Dinner came, and except when Mrs Robert looked at her husband's head she continued gay and flippant, chiding Elizabeth for the profusion on the table, and absolutely protesting against the entrance of the roast turkey, which formed the only exception to 'You see your dinner'. 'I do beg and entreat that no turkey may be seen today. I am really frightened out of my wits with the number of dishes we have already. Let us have no turkey, I beseech you.'

'My dear,' replied Elizabeth, 'the turkey is roasted, and it may just as well come in as stay in the kitchen. Besides, if it is cut, I am in hopes my father may be tempted to eat a bit, for it is rather a favourite dish.'

'You may have it in my dear, but I assure you I shan't touch it.'

Mr Watson had not been well enough to join the party at dinner, but was prevailed on to come down and drink tea with them.

'I wish we may be able to have a game of cards tonight,' said Elizabeth to Mrs Robert, after seeing her father comfortably seated in his armchair.

'Not on my account, my dear, I beg. You know I am no card player. I think a snug chat infinitely better. I always say cards are very well sometimes, to break a formal circle, but one never wants them among friends.'

'I was thinking of its being something to amuse my father,' answered Elizabeth, 'if it was not disagreeable to you. He says his head won't bear whist, but perhaps if we make a round game he may be tempted to sit down with us.'

'By all means, my dear creature. I am quite at your service, only do not oblige me to choose the game, that's all. Speculation is the only round game at Croydon now, but I can play anything. When there is only one or two of you at home, you must be quite at a loss to amuse him – why do not you get him to play at cribbage? Margaret and I have played at cribbage most nights that we have not been engaged.'

A sound like a distant carriage was at this moment caught; everybody listened; it became more decided; it certainly drew nearer. It was an unusual sound in Stanton at any time of the day, for the village was on no very public road, and contained no gentleman's family but the rector's. The wheels rapidly approached; in two minutes the general expectation was answered; they stopped beyond a doubt at the garden gate of the parsonage.

'Who could it be?' – it was certainly a postchaise. Penelope was the only creature to be thought of. She might perhaps have met with some unexpected opportunity of returning. A pause of suspense ensued. Steps were distinguished, first along the paved footway which led under the windows of the house to the front door, and then within the passage. They were the steps of a man. It could not be Penelope. It must be Samuel.

The door opened, and displayed Tom Musgrave in the wrap of a traveller. He had been in London and was now on his way home, and he had come half a mile out of his road merely to call for ten minutes at Stanton. He loved to take people by surprise, with sudden visits at extraordinary seasons, and in the present instance had had the additional motive of being able to tell the Miss Watsons, whom he depended on finding sitting quietly employed after tea, that he was going home to an eight o'clock dinner.

As it happened, however, he did not give more surprise than he received, when instead of being shown into the usual little sitting room, the door of the best parlour, a foot larger each way than the other, was thrown open, and he beheld a circle of smart people whom he could not immediately recognise arranged with all the honours of visiting round the fire, and Miss Watson sitting at the best Pembroke table, with the best tea things before her. He stood for a few seconds, in silent amazement.

'Musgrave!' ejaculated Margaret in a tender voice.

He recollected himself, and came forward, delighted to find such a circle of friends, and blessing his good fortune for the unlooked-for indulgence. He shook hands with Robert, bowed and smiled to the ladies, and did everything very prettily, but as to any particularity of address or emotion towards Margaret, Emma, who closely observed him, perceived nothing that did not justify Elizabeth's opinions, though Margaret's modest smiles imported that she meant to take the visit to herself.

He was persuaded without much difficulty to throw off his greatcoat and drink tea with them. For whether he dined at eight or nine, as he observed, 'was a matter of very little consequence'; and without seeming to seek, he did not turn away from the chair close to Margaret which she was assiduous in providing him. She had thus secured him from her sisters, but it was not immediately in her power to preserve him from her brother's claims, for as he came avowedly from London, and had left it only four hours ago, the last current report as to public news and the general opinion of the day must be understood, before Robert could let his attention be yielded to the less national and important demands of the women.

At last, however, he was at liberty to hear Margaret's soft address, as she spoke her fears of his having had a most terrible, cold, dark, dreadful journey.

'Indeed, you should not have set out so late.'

'I could not be earlier,' he replied. 'I was detained chatting at the Bedford, by a friend. All hours are alike to me. How long have you been in the country, Miss Margaret?'

'We came only this morning. My kind brother and sister brought me home this very morning. 'Tis singular, is not it?'

'You were gone a great while, were not you? A fortnight, I suppose?'

'*You* may call a fortnight a great while, Mr Musgrave,' said Mrs Robert smartly, 'but *we* think a month very little. I assure you we bring her home at the end of a month, much against our will.'

'A month! Have you really been gone a month! 'tis amazing how time flies.'

'You may imagine,' said Margaret in a sort of whisper, 'what are my sensations at finding myself once more at Stanton. You know what a sad visitor I make. And I was so excessively impatient to see Emma; I dreaded the meeting, and at the same time longed for it. Do you not comprehend the sort of feeling?'

'Not at all!' cried he aloud. 'I could never dread a meeting with Miss Emma Watson – or any of her sisters.'

It was lucky that he added that finish.

'Were you speaking to me?' said Emma, who had caught her own name.

'Not absolutely,' he answered, 'but I was thinking of you, as many at a greater distance are probably doing at this moment. Fine open weather, Miss Emma! Charming season for hunting.'

'Emma is delightful, is not she?' whispered Margaret. 'I have found her more than answer my warmest hopes. Did you ever see anything more perfectly beautiful? I think even *you* must be a convert to a brown complexion.'

He hesitated; Margaret was fair herself, and he did not particularly want to compliment her; but Miss Osborne and Miss Carr were likewise fair, and his devotion to them carried the day.

'Your sister's complexion,' said he at last, 'is as fine as a dark complexion can be, but I still profess my preference of a white skin. You have seen Miss Osborne? – she is my model for a truly feminine complexion, and she is very fair.'

51

'Is she fairer than me?'

Tom made no reply.

'Upon my honour, ladies,' said he, giving a glance over his own person, 'I am highly indebted to your condescension for admitting me in such *deshabille* into your drawing room. I really did not consider how unfit I was to be here, or I hope I should have kept my distance. Lady Osborne would tell me that I were growing as careless as her son, if she saw me in this condition

The ladies were not wanting in civil returns, and Robert Watson, stealing a view of his own head in an opposite glass, said with equal civility:

'You cannot be more in *deshabille* than myself. We got here so late, that I had not time even to put a little fresh powder in my hair.'

Emma could not help entering into what she supposed her sister-in-law's feelings at that moment.

When the tea things were removed, Tom began to talk of his carriage, but the old card table being set out, and the fish and counters with a tolerably clean pack brought forward from the beaufit by Miss Watson, the general voice was so urgent with him to join their party that he agreed to allow himself another quarter of an hour. Even Emma was pleased that he would stay, for she was beginning to feel that a family party might be the worst of all parties, and the others were delighted.

'What's your game?' cried he, as they stood round the table.

'Speculation, I believe,' said Elizabeth. 'My sister recommends it, and I fancy we all like it. I know *you* do, Tom.'

'It is the only round game played at Croydon now,' said Mrs Robert, 'we never think of any other. I am glad it is a favourite with you.'

'Oh, me!' cried Tom. 'Whatever you decide on, will be a favourite with *me*. I have had some pleasant hours at speculation in my time, but I have not been in the way of it now for a long while. Vingt-un is the game at Osborne Castle; I have played nothing but vingt-un of late. You would be astonished to hear the noise we make there. The fine old lofty drawing-room rings again. Lady Osborne sometimes declares she cannot hear herself speak. Lord Osborne enjoys it famously – he makes the best dealer without exception that I ever beheld – such quickness and spirit! he lets nobody dream over their cards. I wish you could see him overdraw himself on both his own cards – it is worth anything in the world!'

'Dear me!' cried Margaret, 'why should not we play at vingt-un? I think it is a much better game than Speculation. I cannot say I am very fond of Speculation.'

Mrs Robert offered not another word in support of the game. She was quite vanquished, and the fashions of Osborne Castle carried it over the fashions of Croydon.

'Do you see much of the parsonage family at the Castle, Mr Musgrave?' asked Emma, as they were taking their seats.

'Oh! yes – they are almost always there. Mrs Blake is a nice little good-humoured woman, she and I are sworn friends, and Howard's a very gentleman-like good sort of fellow! You are not forgotten, I assure you, by any of the party. I fancy you must have a little cheek-glowing now and then, Miss Emma. Were you not rather warm last Saturday about nine or ten o'clock in the evening? I will tell you how it was. I see you are dying to know. Says Howard to Lord Osborne...'

At this interesting moment he was called on by the others to regulate the game and determine some disputable point, and his attention was so totally engaged in the business and afterwards by the course of the game as never to revert to what he had been saying before, and Emma, though suffering a good deal from curiosity, dared not remind him.

He proved a very useful addition to their table, without him it would have been a party of such very near relations as could have felt little interest, and perhaps maintained little complaisance, but his presence gave variety and secured good manners.

He was in fact excellently qualified to shine at a round game, and few situations made him appear to greater advantage. He played with spirit and had a great deal to say, and though with no wit himself, could sometimes make use of wit of an absent friend, and had a lively way of retailing a commonplace, or saying a mere nothing, that had great effect at a card table. The ways and good jokes of Osborne Castle were now added to his ordinary means of entertainment; he repeated the smart sayings of one lady, detailed the oversights of another, and indulged them even with a copy of Lord Osborne's style of overdrawing himself on both cards.

The clock struck nine while he was thus agreeably occupied, and when Nanny came in with her master's basin of gruel, he had the pleasure of observing to Mr Watson that he should leave him at supper, while he went home to dinner himself. The carriage was ordered to the door, and no entreaties for his staying longer could now avail, for he well knew that if he stayed he must sit down to supper in less than ten minutes, which to a man whose heart had long been fixed on calling his next meal a dinner was quite insupportable.

On finding him determined to go, Margaret began to wink and nod at Elizabeth to ask him to dinner for the following day, and Elizabeth at last, not able to resist hints which her own hospitable, social temper more than half seconded, gave the invitation.

'Would he give Robert the meeting? they should be very happy.'

'With the greatest pleasure,' was his first reply. In a moment afterwards: 'That is, if I can possibly get here in time, but I shoot with Lord Osborne, and therefore must not engage. You will not think of me unless you see me.'

And so he departed, delighted with the uncertainty in which he had left it.

## Chapter Five

MARGARET, IN THE JOY of her heart under circumstances which she chose to consider as peculiarly propitious, would willingly have made a confidante of Emma when they were alone for a short time the next morning; and had proceeded so far as to say, 'The young man who was here last night, my dear Emma, and returns today, is more interesting to me than perhaps you may be aware...' but Emma, pretending to understand nothing extraordinary in the words, made some very inapplicable reply, and jumping up, ran away from a subject which was odious to her feelings.

As Margaret would not allow a doubt to be repeated of Musgrave's coming to dinner, preparations were made for his entertainment much exceeding what had been deemed necessary the day before, and taking the office of superintendence entirely from her sister, she was half the morning in the kitchen herself, directing and scolding. After a great deal of indifferent cooking and anxious suspense, however, they were obliged to sit down without their guest. Tom Musgrave never came, and Margaret was at no pains to conceal her vexation under the disappointment, or repress the peevishness of her temper.

The peace of the party for the remainder of that day, and the whole of the next, which comprised the length of Robert and Jane's visit, was continually invaded by her fretful displeasure and querulous attacks. Elizabeth was the usual object of both. Margaret had just respect enough for her brother and sister's opinion to behave properly by *them,* but Elizabeth and the maids could never do anything right, and Emma, whom she seemed no longer to think about, found the continuance of the gentle voice beyond her calculation short. Eager to be as little among them as possible, Emma was delighted with the alternative of sitting above with her father, and warmly entreated to be his constant companion each evening – and as Elizabeth loved company of any kind too well not to prefer being below, at all risks, as she had rather talk of Croydon to Jane, with every interruption of Margaret's perverseness, than sit with only her father, who frequently could not endure talking at all, the affair was so settled, as soon as she could be persuaded to believe it no sacrifice on her sister's part. To Emma, the exchange was most acceptable and delightful. Her father, if ill, required little more than gentleness and silence, and, being a man of sense and education, was, if able to converse, a welcome companion.

In *his* chamber, Emma was at peace from the dreadful mortifications of unequal society and family discord – from the immediate endurance of hard-hearted prosperity, low-minded conceit, and wrong-headed folly, engrafted on an untoward disposition. She still suffered from them in the contemplation of their existence, in memory and in prospect, but for the moment she ceased to be tortured by their effects. She was at leisure, she could read and think, though her situation was hardly such as to make reflection very soothing. The evils arising from the loss of her uncle were neither trifling, nor likely to lessen, and when thought had been freely indulged, in contrasting the past and the present, the employment of mind, the dissipation of unpleasant ideas which only reading could produce, made her thankfully turn to a book.

The change in her home society and style of life, in consequence of the death of one friend and the imprudence of another, had indeed been striking. From being the first object of hope and solicitude of an uncle who had formed her mind with the care of a parent, and of tenderness to an aunt whose amiable temper had delighted to give her every indulgence, from being the life and spirit of a house where all had been comfort and elegance, and the expected heiress of an easy independence, she was become of importance to no one, a burden on those whose affection she could not expect, an addition in a house already overstocked, surrounded by inferior minds with little chance of domestic comfort, and as little hope of future support. It was well for her that she was naturally cheerful, for the change had been such as might have plunged weak spirits in despondence.

She was very much pressed by Robert and Jane to return with them to Croydon, and had some difficulty in getting a refusal accepted, as they thought too highly of their own kindness and situation to suppose the offer could appear in a less advantageous light to anybody else. Elizabeth gave them her interest, though evidently against her own, in privately urging Emma to go.

'You do not know what you refuse, Emma,' said she, 'nor what you have to bear at home. I would advise you by all means to accept the invitation; there is always something lively going on at Croydon, you will be in company almost every day, and Robert and Jane will be very kind to you. As for me, I shall be no worse off without you than I have been used to be, but poor Margaret's disagreeable ways are new to *you*, and they would vex you more than you think for, if you stay at home.'

Emma was of course uninfluenced, except to greater esteem for Elizabeth, by such representations, and the visitors departed without her.

## Chapter Six

THE MORNING AFTER Mr and Mrs Robert Watson had gone, Emma received a note from Mrs Blake inviting her to spend the following day at Wickstead Parsonage. 'Charles talks of you a great deal,' she wrote, 'and we should also be happy to see one of your sisters, if it is possible for you to leave Mr Watson.'

There was not very much doubt about which sister to take. While Elizabeth was almost afraid to speak to anybody connected with Osborne Castle, Margaret would never willingly forgo any party of pleasure. After breakfast, then, the two younger Miss Watsons took the cart and set out to drive the four mile distance, the weather promising a cold, but bright day.

Emma remembered so little of the country which she had left fourteen years before that it was necessary for Margaret to direct her. They drove for a considerable time past the wall of Osborne Park, which was sheltered from public gaze by a band of trees, while the elder sister talked almost without a pause of Tom Musgrave.

'He is very shy, Emma – perhaps uncertain of my feelings, for you know it would be immodest of me to show them *too* plainly. That I am convinced is the sole reason why he has not yet made me an offer. But if he happens to know we are going to Wickstead, he may find a reason to call in.'

Emma answered civilly, but as she could hardly think of anybody *less* shy than Tom Musgrave, and foresaw no happiness for Margaret in that quarter, she hoped not to be obliged to meet him again. She contented herself with looking at the countryside they passed, which, though less hilly than Shropshire, she thought had several quiet beauties of its own. Soon they arrived at the village of Wickstead, on the edge of Osborne Park, and came upon a duck pond, a cluster of thatched cottages, a small church with an ancient group of lancet windows and, nearby, a solid, ivy-covered building, the Parsonage. Charles and his sister Caroline, a girl of eight, were playing in the garden with their hoops and ran up to greet them.

'I am *so* glad to meet you again, Miss Emma,' Charles said breathlessly, 'and so will my uncle be, when he comes back from his cottage visiting.'

Mrs Blake received them kindly and, having met her two youngest children, boys of six and five, they sat down to drink tea in the little sitting room. The house was neat and comfortable, though with no particular signs of wealth, and the park with its great trees and sweeping lawns offered a remarkably pleasant prospect. Margaret was soon in raptures over the children and the view.

'So you have lived in Stanton for a long time, Miss Margaret?' Mrs Blake enquired of her.

'Fourteen years,' said Margaret, 'almost all my life, but for most of that time Emma has been far away, so that I hardly know my own dear sister.'

She sighed affectedly.

Emma was unsure how much of her story was known, or what it might have gained in the telling. 'My mother died,' she explained, 'very soon after we came to Stanton, and her sister, my Aunt Turner, took me in, as she and her husband had no family. I lived with them for several years in Shropshire, but–'

'Uncle Turner died,' Margaret broke in, 'and our aunt met a complete stranger, a Captain O'Brien, at Ludlow Assembly – within four weeks they were married – and now they are gone into Ireland and poor Emma is sent back to us without a six-pence. Is not that shocking, Mrs Blake?'

Emma was embarrassed to have their family affairs exposed to strangers. 'It was not as bad as it sounds,' she said, 'my aunt had fully intended that I should go with them, but Captain O'Brien would not consent; by this time they were married and she was obliged to fall in with his wishes. Pray do not judge her harshly, Mrs Blake.'

'But an old woman like that!' cried Margaret.

'She may seem very old to two young ladies like you,' said Mrs Blake, 'but Mrs O'Brien, I understand, is not much beyond forty; she had lost her husband and believed, perhaps, that Miss Emma might soon leave her for a home of her own. Is it so surprising, then, that she should lose her heart to an attractive stranger? *I* have my children to occupy me, but other women, suddenly left alone, may be very tempted to snatch at any prospect of happiness. And, perhaps, when you yourself are forty, you will not think it such a great age.'

'She is forty-*eight*!' Margaret said.

The children were growing restless, and now asked that the visitors should come out with them to see the stables and garden. Mrs Blake said, 'You shall go, Miss Margaret, while your sister and I wash the china.'

Emma was thankful to have a few minutes without Margaret. She and Mrs Blake were already good friends and, as they washed and dried the old blue Wedgwood cups, found themselves talking quite familiarly.

'We have lived here these last five years,' her hostess said. 'My husband died – most suddenly, most unexpectedly – when Frank was a baby, and we were left with almost nothing. See how helpless we women are, Miss Emma! I would rather have gone out as a governess than be a burden on John – my brother – but the children must have bread and an education. I try to keep a comfortable home for him; *that*, at least, is in my power.'

'Mr Howard seems very fond of Charles,' said Emma.

'He is. He has never complained. He was a Fellow of St John's College, Oxford, several years ago, but fellows are not allowed to marry, you know, and I don't think that would have suited him. He became Lord Osborne's tutor, for they could do nothing with that young man at Eton, and was actually living at the Castle when I was widowed. At once he told the family that he must leave – take any job he could get, so that he could provide a home for me and my children. But since the Osbornes were not at all willing to part with him, they offered him this house and the charge of Wickstead. The gentleman who was here before him was given another living in Kent.'

Several livings to dispose of, thought Emma; what *very* rich people the Osbornes must be.

'And here he comes this moment,' Mrs Blake added cheerfully. 'I always know, because the children are so glad to see him.'

Mr Howard came into the kitchen, surrounded by a group of talking little boys and Margaret. Emma thought him quite as handsome as when she had first met him. He was tall, with a pleasant open countenance and hair cut short in the modern style, and said something, as they shook hands, about having had the happiness of meeting her father.

'Uncle John,' cried little Charles, 'may we take our visitors to the park, so I can ride my horse?'

This horse – a present from the Osborne family – was saddled, and they passed through a small wicket gate which led from the end of the garden into the park. Emma thought it even more delightful at close quarters. The day was fine; a few deer wandered among the great elms and oaks now touched with yellow, and the little boys ran around looking for the last horse chestnuts, while the adults talked and Charles rode alongside.

'I had my Latin lesson first thing this morning! *Amo, amas, amat* – Do you know what that means, Miss Emma?

'I think so,' Emma said, laughing. 'I picked up a little Latin in my uncle's house.'

'And I can say *mensa, mensam,*' cried little Frank, 'but it is very tedious.'

'It does not come easily,' Mr Howard said, 'and many things interest my nephews more than the Romans, but I am afraid they must persist, or they may have a hard time when they go out in the world.'

Emma thought he was touching on the family's lack of fortune, and said, to change the subject, 'You were Lord Osborne's tutor, were you not?'

'Yes, I taught him for a year before he went to Oxford, but—' He broke off, and Emma wondered if he had been about to say that Lord Osborne had been far from an apt pupil. 'I hesitated,' he went on, 'for, as Harriet has probably told you, our family is very little used to mixing with the nobility. But Lord Osborne has the power to do so much good, in Parliament and on his estates, that I judged it wrong to refuse. And afterwards— There, how do you like that, Miss Emma?'

They had come within sight of Osborne Castle, a fine building almost twice the size of Emma's former home in Shropshire, with three long lines of windows. Margaret was perfectly astonished and gasped, 'Well, I have never seen so great a house in all my life!'

'I've been inside lots of times,' Charles said, 'and look, there is Lady Osborne!'

The lady strolling on the terrace gestured to them to come near, and they walked across the grass into the shadow of the castle, which was approached by an avenue of lime trees on the western side. Emma, seeing her for the first time in daylight, was very much struck with Lady Osborne. She was tall for a woman, with brilliant blue eyes and a great deal of light-coloured hair, and her voice when she addressed them was low and caressing.

'Miss Emma Watson – I remember you well – and I am also happy to meet Miss Margaret. You have not been inside the castle, I believe – will you not take some refreshment?'

Mrs Blake declined, with many thanks, saying that her younger children needed to rest, but Mr Howard, the Miss Watsons and Charles followed her into the castle, having first handed over the horse to a groom. Emma had been inside a few great houses, but none that could compare with this one. She observed some very fine Canalettos and Gainsboroughs in the hall – and Charles was not slow to point out the stuffed badger; they then entered her ladyship's private parlour, which overlooked an artificial lake gleaming in the sun.

Among the many portraits in this room were one of Lady Osborne as a bride, by Romney, and a companion picture of the late lord, who looked very like his son. Emma would have found it almost impossible to believe that this lady was the mother of two grown children, had not the same young people very shortly joined them, as a servant brought in China tea.

The Honourable Fanny Osborne was smaller and plainer than her mother; her manners cold and careless. Having cast a scornful eye over the modest costumes of Emma and Margaret, she said little. Her brother slouched in after her, and his eyes immediately went to the youngest Miss Watson. He placed himself in the chair next to hers and said without preamble, 'My head is so bad, after last night, I did not feel well enough to go hunting.'

'I am sorry to hear it, my lord.'

'Musgrave and I sat half the night over a quart of sherry,' he went on, 'and I am quite done up. Well, at least I have the pleasure of seeing *you*.' Emma knew not what to say. 'I looked for you at Stanton Wood the other day, but you weren't there. Would you not like to see the hunt in full cry, Miss Emma?'

Emma replied tactfully that she had never seen it.

'Some people don't share your tastes, Reginald,' Miss Osborne said languidly; 'there is Mr Howard, for instance, who will not hunt.'

'Won't you?' asked Margaret, who was sitting next to him and evidently very much in awe of the great people.

'No,' Mr Howard said calmly. 'I had rather observe a beautiful bird or stag than kill it.'

'I understand your feelings, Mr Howard,' said Lady Osborne in her charming voice, 'and it is many years since I have hunted. No, Reginald, I don't want to hear any more about it! Now, would you all care for some music?'

Emma had not touched the pianoforte since her return to Surrey, for the Watson family possessed none, but she had had the benefit of excellent masters in Shropshire, and was happy to play a little. Miss Osborne rattled through a tune or two, and then her mother played a short, but exquisite air, singing in French almost as though it were her native language.

'That is very fine,' Mr Howard said, 'your ladyship's accent is flawless.'

'It brings back many memories,' Lady Osborne said softly, 'for you know' – to Emma and Margaret – 'I was brought up in France, before the Revolution – and left it only when I was married, almost as a child.'

Shortly afterwards it was time to return to the Parsonage, and they left, with many thanks for their entertainment. Margaret was loud in her praises of the Castle, the grounds, and their hostess, but Mrs Blake, to whom these were chiefly addressed, only said quietly that the Osbornes had been very kind to their family.

## Chapter Seven

AFTER A PLEASANT dinner at the Parsonage, the young ladies began to stir, as it was growing dark. Mr Howard said he would ride back with them and pay his respects to Mr Watson, and they parted most affectionately from the children and Mrs Blake.

Emma drove down the narrow leaf-fringed lanes, in the greyish twilight, while Mr Howard rode alongside. He pointed out the early stars: 'And there,' he said, 'is a very fine sight – Mars, a remarkably deep red, and closer to earth than usual.'

'La!' cried Margaret, 'I am sure I am not clever enough to understand astronomy.'

'But why not, Miss Margaret?' Mr Howard enquired. 'Not because you are a woman, I am sure; I have met a lady, Miss Caroline Herschel, who is almost as good an astronomer as her brother.'

Margaret could think of nothing to say.

Arrived at Stanton, he went briefly to Mr Watson, who was in bed, but happy to talk a little, then, after a few kind remarks to Elizabeth, took his leave. Margaret was in such good spirits and had had such a pleasant day, that she could almost forgive him for not being Tom Musgrave.

'Well, girls,' cried Elizabeth, 'fancy your being received at the Castle itself! I want to hear what it was like, Margaret; the pictures, and the gardens, and what you had to drink, and everything. Did you say that it was real China tea?'

Margaret assured her that it was. She had been almost ready, at first, to drop down dead with fright, but the Osbornes were so affable and condescending, they had treated them almost as if they were their equals.

'And Mr Howard is very agreeable, is he not?' said Elizabeth, in high good humour. 'I did not expect him to trouble to speak to me.'

Margaret said solemnly, when she had sat down:

'Miss Fanny Osborne is in love with him!'

'Do you think so, Margaret?' asked Emma. 'I could see no sign of it, and her family, I think, would expect her to look a little higher than a country parson, and marry someone of her own rank.'

'You only say so because you like him yourself, Emma,' Margaret retorted, 'and, depend upon it, they would not show all those favours to the Blakes, and give a horse to the little boy, without some good reason. Lady Osborne would probably be very glad to get him for her daughter; she was hanging on his words the whole time.'

Emma was silenced, but she recalled that Miss Osborne had talked and danced only with officers at the White Hart ball, and she knew, as Margaret probably did not, that Mr Howard had no private fortune. The styles of living at castle and parsonage were so very different that she could not believe any such marriage was contemplated. And perhaps she did not wish to believe it either, for certainly the brother and sister, great people or not, seemed to her much inferior to Mr Howard.

Two days later, and this time at a more convenient hour, Lord Osborne and Tom Musgrave again called for thirty minutes. Elizabeth was in the kitchen making crab apple jelly, and could not be persuaded to join them. Emma would rather not have been there, but both gentlemen distinguished her so particularly that she had no possibility of getting away. She thought Lord Osborne slower and more stupid than ever. Why he came, she knew not, as he had no conversation, but merely stared at her a great deal and made some very dull remarks. However, Tom rattled on for so long and paid her so many compliments that Margaret could not conceal her anger as soon as the gentlemen had gone. The sweet smile disappeared, and she rounded on her sister.

'I do think, Emma, it is very unkind of you to engross Tom Musgrave to yourself when you know that he is my particular friend. I call it very unnatural in my own sister. To be sure, Penelope has done the same thing – that is why Elizabeth is an old maid – but I did not expect it from *you*! You are younger – you can wait your turn – and I assure you, he means nothing by his nonsense and compliments, since that is the way he talks to all the young women!'

Shocked and wounded, Emma could not help wishing that Margaret would apply her good advice to herself.

'Upon my honour, Margaret, even if I liked a man I should never try to take him away from one of my sisters. It would be wrong; I could not be at ease if I did it. And besides, I do *not* have any particular liking for Tom Musgrave. You may refuse to believe me, but it is so.'

'Do leave her alone, Margaret,' said Elizabeth, who had entered the room in her apron just in time for the last remark. 'Emma is a really good little creature, she is not your enemy, and I am afraid Tom Musgrave is more interested in the young women at the Castle than in her or you.'

Soon afterwards they had a much more welcome visitor, their brother Sam, who rode over from Guildford on one of his few free days. Emma was delighted with him. He was a good-looking young fellow of two-and-twenty, not very well dressed and looking thin and fagged, but most unaffectedly pleased to meet his youngest sister once more. 'I should have known you anywhere, Emma,' he assured her. Mr Watson was well enough to come downstairs and the family sat down to a comfortable dinner.

'By the way, father,' said he when Nanny was bringing in the stewed plums, 'I saw an old friend of Robert's yesterday – Mr Purvis, who has the living of Alford about fourteen miles off. I was called in when one of his children had a throat infection, and he asked how you all did.'

'How does he look?' Elizabeth asked, in a faint voice.

'Quite old. Nearer forty than thirty. I had trouble remembering who he was.'

'No, he is only thirty-two,' Elizabeth protested, but Sam did not hear. Emma could see that she was very much moved.

After they had got up, 'Will you forgive me, sir, if I leave straight away? – there are some people in the town that I ought to see.'

'He means Mary Edwards,' said Elizabeth as Sam rode off down the dirty lane. 'Poor boy; I suppose he will not believe it until he hears it from her own lips. Well, Emma, you have now met all your brothers and sisters, except Penelope – I cannot think what she is doing. It is three weeks since she wrote home.' She continued with a sigh, 'I was afraid I should faint when Sam mentioned James Purvis. He was a schoolboy at the time and did not observe what was going on. It is very wicked to think of him, is it not? – I should so like to see his children. Well, we are never likely to meet now, with him in Alford and me here, and it is just as well, because he would be very disappointed to see how I have gone off.'

Emma perceived that her sister was really wounded, and felt more than ever ashamed of the conduct of Penelope, who had now been gone from home for two months.

## Chapter Eight

A DARK TIME now began for the family, for on the day after Sam's visit Mr Watson awoke very languid. He was in no pain, but over the next fortnight appeared to grow a little weaker every day. The physician who called regularly told Elizabeth that he did not expect him to last until Christmas.

Emma sat with him for hours each day, often reading from his favourite Crabbe's *Tales*. Towards evening his mind would wander, and he sometimes spoke of the time when, as a girl of five, she had left Stanton.

'It seemed such an unnatural thing, my dear Emma, to send a child away from her home, but you were so very young – you had no mother – and Mr Turner and Sophy were so fond of you. Poor Sophy, I wonder how she is doing. I hesitated – Shropshire is a long way off – but Robert pointed out that they could give you a far more comfortable home than we could. For myself I am not sorry to go, but I should have liked to see you girls married. Robert was always sensible, even as a boy – Robert will look after you...'

'Dear father,' said Emma soothingly, though not perhaps very truthfully, 'I feel sure that we brothers and sisters will each do everything we can for the other's good.'

As the days went on she thought much of the family she had lost – her mother, of whom she had only the faintest remembrance; her father, an active man of middle age when she left home, but now white-haired and feeble; her brothers and sisters, whom she could not expect to have any particular regard

69

for her after a childhood spent apart. She believed that Sam and Elizabeth would always be her friends, but Robert and Margaret evidently thought her a burden, and she could have little confidence in Penelope's good humour. The time passed slowly. The incumbent of the next parish, Mr Grant, called once or twice, but that was of little comfort because all knew that he would succeed to the living when it became vacant. He had five children, and naturally wished for an increase of income. Robert came one day, without his wife, and seemed in low spirits. It was clear to him that he might have to provide for his sisters rather sooner than had been expected. Sam also rode over for a few hours, and confirmed the doctor's opinion that the end could not now be long delayed.

The weather turned dull, with several days of driving rain. Margaret's temper was not improved by a note from the Edwardses, saying they supposed that the Miss Watsons could not now think of coming to the November assembly. 'I do not see what good it does for me or anyone to stay at home,' she complained. She spent most of her time looking out of the window at the dripping laurels and doing very little to help Nanny and Elizabeth, who were run off their feet.

Emma tried to get a short walk each day, wrapping up well and putting on pattens to avoid the deep mud. Dismal as the climate was outside, it was less melancholy than within the house, which would soon be theirs no longer. One morning she met Mr Howard and he dismounted and walked beside her to the door.

'I am just going to read Herodotus with your father,' he said, 'for you know we Oxford men think nothing is any good unless it is in a dead language.' And on leaving: 'It is *your* loss, Miss Emma, not his – but my sister and I will help in any way we can.'

Throughout this time there came absolutely no word from Penelope. They had received a note, the very day that Mr Watson was taken ill, telling of a walk around the cathedral gardens with Dr Harding, but no more. Elizabeth had informed her of their father's declining health, and a little later Emma took it upon herself to write again, telling her plainly that she must soon come home, if she wished to see him alive. To this, also, there was no reply.

Emma could not understand it. Her sister might, perhaps, have difficulty finding someone to bring her from Chichester, but she felt that she herself would have gone in the public coach, rather than keep away. There was certainly nothing to stop her corresponding. Elizabeth shook her head wearily when she remarked on it. 'She is trying to fix Dr Harding,' she said, and would say no more.

The end came peacefully on a rainy night in the third week of November. Over the next few days almost the entire family gathered at Stanton; Robert, Jane and Sam, who was obliged to leave immediately after the funeral. There was constant talk among all who were there about what Penelope could be at.

Once the coffin had been carried from the small Norman church over a path strewn with damp and rotting leaves Mr Howard, who had assisted at the service, shook hands with Robert and Elizabeth and repeated his good wishes. Back at home, Emma found it hard to endure the conduct of some of her family. Jane roamed about the house, looked inside cupboards, and helped herself to a set of apostle spoons which she had long coveted, complaining as she did so that the furniture was old-fashioned, and would all have to go.

Robert was resigned. 'Well, I suppose you girls will have to come back to Croydon. We have two very good bedrooms, and Elizabeth can go in Gussy's little cupboard, but I don't know what we shall do with Penelope, when she condescends to show herself again.'

Emma dreaded the prospect. Jane's manners, and his own, showed very clearly how little they relished the thought of having four extra persons in their house.

She went upstairs to the room which she shared with Elizabeth and began composing a letter to her aunt in Ireland. There was an awkwardness in writing to her, after what had passed, but she thought it right to inform her of Mr Watson's death and to ask for her news. She had only just sealed it when Nanny brought a note from Mrs Blake; this urged her most kindly to come to Wickstead for a little change, after her home should be broken up.

She had not yet begun a reply when there came a sound of wheels. Emma looked out of the window and saw a smart carriage approaching in the rain; it stopped, and out got two ladies and an elderly gentleman. Thinking that this might be Penelope at last she ran downstairs and a few minutes later found herself tenderly embraced by her sister.

'My little Emma! How many years since we have met! I am so sorry, Elizabeth,' she went on, 'to have missed seeing our father at the last, but we had gone to London on a jaunt, and all your letters arrived in a great heap the other day. Dear old man, there is no expressing how I shall miss him! And now I have some news which will surprise you very much – Dr Harding and I are to be married!'

The faces of Mr and Mrs Robert Watson brightened perceptibly at this important news. Only three sisters to support, instead of four! When the introductions had been made, and cake and wine brought by Nanny, Emma was at leisure to study their visitors.

Penelope Watson looked not unlike Margaret, being fair, with strongly-marked features, and although at six-and-twenty she was three years older, had the better appearance of the two. Her manners were decided, almost bold, and the black ribbons she was wearing for her father could not conceal her obvious good spirits. Dr Harding was a stout gentleman in a white wig with a purple complexion. Emma understood that he had a stall at Chichester cathedral and two rich livings in Sussex. The third person was his widowed daughter Mrs Monks, a little sour-faced woman in her middle thirties, who appeared none too pleased at the prospect of a stepmother fully ten years younger than herself.

'Dr Harding has a fine house in the Close,' said Penelope, 'where he lives with dear Louisa' – a nod to the silent Mrs Monks. 'We shall all be so happy. I had intended to come home for a short while, Elizabeth, but as you will soon all be moving out, I shall stay on with my friends in Chichester until we are married, and that will be the week before Christmas.'

'Aye, no point wasting time,' Dr Harding asserted abruptly.

'Will you give me away, dear Robert?' Penelope asked. 'It is to be a *very* quiet wedding, but I should so like to have all my family around me.'

'With the greatest pleasure,' said Robert, 'and I dare say, Dr Harding, when you are settled, you will like to have one or two of my sisters to stay with you. Chichester is a fine place for young ladies to catch husbands, it seems!'

'No, no,' Dr Harding said in haste, 'it's Penny I am marrying, not her family. No, Mr Watson; your sisters are your own business, not mine. I can't have my house filled with silly women, gossiping and getting under my feet.'

Tears sprang into Elizabeth's eyes, and the conversation faltered. As it was beginning to be dark, Penelope soon went to her room to fetch a few belongings, and then the whole party drove off to spend the night at the White Hart. Robert and Jane were loud in their condemnation of the Doctor's bad manners once he was gone, and Emma silently reflected upon Penelope's luck in marrying an ill-natured man of sixty, who had already buried two wives.

Margaret was the most indignant. 'I would not marry a man like that,' she said, ' though he had ten thousand a year.'

'Oh, yes, you would, Margaret,' Jane said sharply, 'and if you did not, I should be very angry with you. Pray remember that you are now wholly dependent on your brother and me, and I am taking bread out of my little girl's mouth to feed you. Penelope has done quite as well as anybody could expect. The man will, probably, be dead in two or three years, and she can then do whatever she likes.'

'I could have done just as well,' lamented Margaret, 'if anyone had invited *me* to Chichester.'

'Then you must find some friends there, Margaret! I am not surprised that you have none, continually complaining as you are.'

Emma thought that there did not seem much prospect of happiness when the three sisters should be obliged to share a home with their brother, and, unable to bear any more, silently left the room.

## Chapter Nine

IT WAS THE NIGHT before the removal. Almost all the family furniture was packed or sold; various oak chairs and antique dressers which Emma faintly remembered from her childhood had been summarily disposed of, along with most of Mr Watson's library, for Robert was not a reading man. Elizabeth and Margaret were to go straight to Croydon, but she had very gladly consented to be the guest of Mrs Blake for a fortnight.

Robert approved highly. 'Mrs Blake has a brother, has she not? Yes, I met him at the funeral. You must see what you can do there, Emma.'

On the Friday evening, he and his wife were dining with an old acquaintance in D., and Elizabeth, worn out, had retired to bed with a headache. Sam called to take a final look at the old home but, after spending a few hours with his sisters, rode off again – they believed, to see the Edwards family.

At eight o' clock the sound of wheels made them suppose that Robert was coming back again, but no such thing – it was Tom Musgrave who presented himself in the parlour, which was now so sadly depleted of pictures and furniture that both girls were embarrassed he should see it. The young man was flushed and with sparkling eyes, which made Emma wonder whether he had been drinking. But he threw himself down in one of the few remaining chairs and said in his ordinary voice, 'Well, ladies, so this is your very last night at home?'

'Our dear old home!' Margaret said with a deep sigh.

'Aye, it's a loss, but perhaps you may come back for a visit, or I may find myself in Croydon, so we needn't quite say good-bye yet.'

Delighted at this hint, Margaret found a half-drunk bottle of parsnip wine and poured him a full glass, which he accepted gratefully. Emma was distressed. She knew her sister wished her to be gone, so after talking a while she made the excuse of fetching tea and stepped out to the kitchen, where she thought she would be safe. But she had not been there five minutes when Tom reappeared and propped himself against a wall, ready for more conversation.

'Going to stay at Wickstead, Miss Emma?'

'Yes, sir. I go tomorrow.'

'Well, perhaps I shall call, and if you are in luck, you may get yourself invited to the Castle. I can tell you in confidence, my friend Osborne admires you. "The beautiful Emma Watson", that's what he said. Lucky fellow, to come into his inheritance when he was but eighteen.'

Margaret followed them out and positioned herself as near to Tom as she dared.

'You may not know,' he continued, 'that the old lord was an invalid for the last ten years of his life and scarcely knew what was going on around him. His wife was younger and grew up in France; that's where she gets her charming manners. Pretty woman, though older than she looks. She was Lady Susan Villiers, daughter of a Whig peer who lived abroad, and had thirty thousand pounds. She filled the Castle and the London house with people of fashion, they had parties night and day and I know for a fact, that she was carrying on an intrigue with Lord Wiltshire, for at least five years while old Osborne lived.'

'How very shocking!' cried Margaret. 'I cannot conceive how a married woman could use her husband so!'

This was said with a languishing look at Tom.

'Can't you, Miss Margaret? Ah, but that's the way with aristocrats; you parsons' daughters don't know what it's like in the big bad world. There's your sister looking disapproving. Have you a lover, Miss Emma?'

'No, sir,' said Emma briskly.

'Too bad – never mind – a pretty girl like you will soon get a whole string. No, Miss Margaret, I am not going to make love to your sister – a higher destiny is reserved for her.' He collapsed on to the stool and blinked.

'Mr Musgrave,' Emma said indignantly, 'this is a house of mourning; if you drink any more you will be too ill to drive home. I will make you a cup of coffee to clear your head and then, perhaps—'

'But pray tell me, Mr Musgrave,' interrupted Margaret, 'is it really true what you say of Lady Osborne? She is a *very* good-looking woman – handsomer than her own daughter – but I am sure that at her time of life...'

Tom answered confidently, 'Don't you believe it, Miss Margaret; that lady has too high a spirit to mind how old she is. Between ourselves, she likes the parson. He goes up to the Castle and talks parish business – dreary stuff – but she has him with her for hours.'

'What! Mr Howard?'

'To be sure. She has showered benefits on him and his family and why would she do that, if she did not like him? It is true,' Tom went on, 'that he is not a bad fellow – keeps his sermons pretty short, so I generally don't wake up until he has done. But I can never really like a man who does not hunt.'

'But surely,' Margaret cried in horror, 'it is not possible that Mr Howard could feel any affection for such an old woman!'

'Affection? Who's talking about that? No, if a man had his choice, he'd naturally prefer a bewitching little thing like Miss Emma or you, but if there is no money in the case, he must shift as he can. Depend upon it, Howard knows which side his bread is buttered. He'll marry her and be thankful – Excuse me, ladies.'

He opened the kitchen door and blundered out into the garden. Margaret, much alarmed, ran after him. There was a bright moon and they soon discerned Tom lying, not fully conscious, on a patch of ground under the mulberry tree. When they asked him how he did, he mumbled something about some negus he had drunk before leaving D., and too much parsnip wine.

'He cannot lie here all night,' Margaret cried, 'he will catch his death!'

The two girls could not shift him, and Emma was about to run into the house to fetch Nanny when their younger brother fortunately rode up and enquired what the matter was. Between the three of them, Tom Musgrave was dragged back into the kitchen, his coat smeared with fresh mud, and Sam knelt on the floor to examine him.

'I am sure that he is really ill!' Margaret exclaimed distractedly. 'Oh, Sam, will he live?'

'I dare say,' said Sam, who seemed very much inclined to laugh; 'I have often seen fellows in this state. But he may have a bad head in the morning.'

He considered. 'If we can get him back in his curricle I'll drive him home; it's a lovely night and I know a man at D. who can give me a bed. Well, this is the great Tom Musgrave! Don't worry, Emma; I shall see you before I go. The White Hart, is it?'

With great difficulty and some assistance from Nanny, Tom was hoisted into his own carriage, and Sam climbed up after him. Emma felt angry that he should have this trouble on his last night at home, and when they saw so little of him; distressed, too, at Margaret's ill-judgement. Soon afterwards she finished packing and went to bed, taking with her some very unpleasant and disturbing thoughts. She knew not whether to believe half of what Tom Musgrave had said, but here, at any rate, was one acquaintance she would not be sorry to leave behind.

## Chapter Ten

THE NEXT MORNING Mr and Mrs Robert Watson left the village taking with them Margaret and Elizabeth, while Mrs Blake carried off Emma and her box to Wickstead Parsonage. Robert was to bring her to Croydon in a fortnight's time, and soon afterwards the whole family would go on to Chichester for Penelope's marriage.

Sam had reached home early, but was obliged to leave again almost at once to attend his employer. 'Write to me, Emma,' he said before going, 'and we shall meet again at Christmas. That's an empty-headed fellow; I hope Margaret does not like him. Well, I have seen Mary Edwards once or twice, but I'm afraid her father and mother are as much against me as ever.' All three sisters were close to tears as they waved him off and quitted Stanton for the last time.

There followed for Emma ten days of almost perfect happiness. She had not thought that she *could* be happy again so soon, but, after the misery of the past few weeks, the cheerful and quiet routine at Wickstead was exactly what was most soothing for her. She had her own comfortable room with a view over Osborne Park, the first time she had slept alone since she quitted Shropshire. The days passed agreeably, teaching and playing with the children, helping their mother in the various household tasks and taking long walks in the park, for the weather had cleared. She felt her affection for the whole family growing daily. Mrs Blake was already a valued friend, and the more she saw of Mr Howard the better she liked him. He was out a good deal about the parish – for he had charge of another village two miles off – but made time to give the boys their lesson each day and told them Greek and Roman stories, many of which were new to Emma. In the evening, while the ladies sewed, he would read to them from Cowper or Miss Edgeworth. Emma knew that his responsibilities to his sister's family had, perhaps, placed it out of his power to marry, yet she never saw any impatience, any loss of temper with the children.

She thought much, of course, about Tom Musgrave's insinuations on the night before she left Stanton. It was true she *wished* them to be false, but setting that aside, she could see no evidence of any close relationship between Mr Howard and Lady Osborne. He called at the Castle on certain days, to inform the family what was going on in the parish and of any cases of need among the cottagers, but he appeared to spend little time there compared with what he spent around the village or at home. Besides, the gap of age, tastes and rank was so great that any marriage seemed out of the question. His manners to Lady Osborne she had already observed. They were quietly kind and civil, as to everyone else, but with no sign of particular regard. She decided that it had been all idle talk on Tom's part.

I am certainly in some danger of falling in love with him, she thought, and I must be careful – it may all die away naturally after I go to Croydon. But there was no doubt of his being the most agreeable man she had met, and whenever they talked at any length she became more certain, that their thoughts, their feelings were alike.

One day she went to the study to call him and Charles for dinner and found him deep in conversation with the little boy.

'It is not Latin, Miss Watson,' he said, 'it is Mr Clarkson's pamphlet on the slave trade. I think it right that Charles should know something of the world before he leaves home and, perhaps, meets people who have made their fortune in that way.'

'I have read it,' Emma said with warm interest.

'You really have?'

'Yes, my uncle told me about the subject as soon as I was able to understand, and he once had a great argument with a Bristol merchant, and turned him out of our house.'

'*My* uncle would turn *me* out,' Charles said, 'if I became a slave trader.'

Mr Howard smiled. 'Yes, Charles will find that not everybody thinks as we do. I hope Lord Osborne will one day take his seat in Parliament and endeavour to do some good, but he seems quite apathetic at present.' This was the nearest he had ever got to a criticism of the Castle family. 'Well, there is still hope while he is young.'

Charles ran out of the room at this point, but Mr Howard did not seem inclined to go; instead he placed a chair for Emma and said, 'I should have liked to know your uncle, Miss Watson; I gather that it was Mr and Mrs Turner who brought you up, and that you have only recently come to Surrey.'

'He was not my uncle by blood,' Emma said, 'but I looked on him as a parent. He was an invalid for several years; perhaps, if it had not been so, he would have made more of a mark in the world. We lived very quietly, but I had the run of his library, which was an excellent one, and he took great pains with my education.'

'So you have lost both your uncle and your father in the last two years,' Mr Howard said. 'That is hard – but your aunt will, I am sure, one day come back to you, and meanwhile you are surrounded by brothers and sisters.' There was a moment's silence; Emma could not say how much in those brothers and sisters she had found to deplore. 'You are fortunate – Harriet and I lost our parents at an early age; we have only some distant cousins, and my brother-in-law, though an amiable man, left his wife and children with almost nothing. They are all the family I have, and, as you see, we are on very good terms.'

'Do you ever regret losing the scholar's life?' Emma asked.

It was strange how intimately they should be talking, yet she felt quite at home in this little room with its book-lined shelves; the bust of Homer on the desk; the trees with their few remaining leaves fluttering outside the window. It reminded her so strongly of her uncle's library in Shropshire that she could almost think the events of the past two years had not occurred.

'Well, I did at first – but it is better as it is. Most young men at Oxford have no interest in books, as I dare say you know, but I always liked them; it would have been quite easy for me to shut myself up in St John's and never come out again. I was strongly tempted to go back there once Lord Osborne was off my hands, but I think it is a more useful life, looking after the parish and teaching Harriet's children. They are bright little things. As the poet says, it's a delightful task, to rear the tender thought –'

'"To teach the young idea how to shoot",' Emma smilingly completed the quotation.

'So you know *The Seasons*,' Mr Howard said. 'I perceive that your uncle's library was indeed a good one, Miss Watson. I don't think Charles will ever be a scholar; he likes the outdoor life too much, but I must lay the foundations.' His face clouded slightly. 'Yes, I must push them on, or I don't know what will become of them; the one thing I can hope to bequeath to those children is a well-stocked mind.'

Charles himself appeared at the door at this point, and asked them if they were never coming to eat their dinner, so the conversation had to be broken off. But over the next few days, Emma and Mr Howard found themselves talking to each other more and more frequently. Mrs Blake certainly observed the growing intimacy between her brother and her young guest, but she seemed, if anything, to encourage it.

One day she said, apropos of nothing, 'I wish that John would marry, Emma; I wish that he could meet some good-humoured, unpretending girl who is not afraid to live on a small income. He never says it, but I cannot help feeling that I and the children are a great burden to him. People think we must be rich because we are so intimately connected with the Osbornes, but we are not.'

'I suppose,' Emma enquired cautiously, 'that he has met various ladies at the Castle.'

'A few. There was a young Lady Flora whom he liked – she resembled you a little, Emma, dark and lively – but that was several years ago, and she is now the wife of another man. I don't think that the quiet life we lead would have suited her, and we certainly would not have been grand enough for her family. But I must not complain. The Osbornes have been very kind to Charles.' And she began to talk of something else.

All this time Emma had not seen Lady Osborne, but one fine day, when Mr Howard had driven them out to see a certain famous view, they met her in her barouche and stopped to talk for a few minutes. The result was an invitation to dine at the Castle the following night.

The plate was Sèvres, the food and wine far finer than Emma had been accustomed to even in her uncle's house. Miss Osborne had returned to London with her friend, unable to bear the country in November, but her brother was there, lumpish and silent as ever. Emma several times caught him staring at her, but he said nothing that was worth hearing.

'I only shot four birds today,' he complained, 'and the fox we caught on Thursday was quite an old one, not strong enough to give us a good run. I may go back to London and see what the fellows are doing, if things don't soon improve.'

Emma was struggling for a reply when she found Lady Osborne's eyes fixed on her.

'So, Miss Watson,' she enquired in her usual soft tones, 'you are not gone to Croydon with the rest of your family?'

Emma explained that Mrs Blake had kindly asked her to stay.

'And I hope she will often come back,' said Mrs Blake, 'for

83

we are great friends, and the children dote on her.'

'Indeed they do,' Mr Howard agreed.

Emma rejoiced to hear this, and to see the smile on Mr Howard's face when he glanced at her. Yet she did not feel quite comfortable in Lady Osborne's presence; she could not explain it, since the older woman had said nothing that was not civil, yet she was uneasy – she longed to be out of her company. I will not, she thought, no, I will *not* be influenced by anything that Tom Musgrave has said. After dinner Lord Osborne said, 'Why don't you play us one of those nice tunes of yours, Miss Watson?' She obliged, but only for a short time, and it was a relief to be able to walk home with her friends under the stars.

It wanted four days of Emma's return to Croydon, when a letter arrived at breakfast-time for Mr Howard.

'I must go to Oxford, Harriet,' he said as soon as he had read it, 'my friend Murray, who was with me at St John's, is very ill. It is serious – a fall from a carriage – and he is not expected to live twenty-four hours.'

'I remember him,' Mrs Blake said, 'of course you must go, John. I will see to everything here.'

Mr Howard was off in half an hour; his sister anxiously urging him to take care. He kissed her, shook Emma's hand and expressed the hope of seeing her before she left, and told the children to be good. There was a sense of vacancy in the house once he was gone.

'Well,' said Mrs Blake, rousing herself, 'I shall give Charles and Caroline their lesson, and why do not you take the little boys for their run? It is such a glorious morning that it will do you all good.'

She gave Emma the key to the park, and they passed through the garden gate. It was very cold, but the sun gleamed brilliantly; the lawns and boughs were thickly covered in frost and the hollies with scarlet fruit. Frank and Henry ran around, whooping with delight each time they saw a squirrel, and Emma walked after them briskly, taking care not to let them get too far away. She had much to think of – Mr Howard galloping down the icy roads, whether he would return before she had to leave, how she would get on in Robert's house. It was growing uncomfortably close to the time when she was expected at Croydon.

Her reflections were interrupted by the sight of Lady Osborne walking in the general direction of the Parsonage, and, although she could not be quite at ease Emma moved forward and greeted her with an artificial smile.

'Good morning,' her ladyship said shortly. 'I expected Mr Howard an hour ago; where is he?.'

'He has just left,' Emma explained, 'for Oxford. He is gone to be with an old friend who is very ill; in fact, dying. I am afraid there was no time to write a note, but Mrs Blake—'

She was startled by the other woman's expression; it was more than disappointment, it looked like anger.

'She should certainly have done so,' Lady Osborne said coldly. 'And when do *you* go?'

'On Friday; my brother has business in the neighbourhood and will take me back with him.'

'Good.' Her ladyship began to walk back along the path towards the Castle and Emma, not well knowing what to do, walked alongside. 'I don't imagine you will come again, Miss Watson; you have already accepted a great deal of hospitality from the parsonage family. Perhaps you are unaware that this is not a public right of way, and I do not allow the common run of people in my park?'

Emma was shocked and confused. Lady Osborne had seen her in the park on her very first visit. They had walked here every day without comment or question. Hardly knowing what to think she replied, 'I am sorry. I understood that the park was open to Mrs Blake and her guests.'

'If I choose, yes. But you are not quite the kind of young

person I wish to see – however, if you are going back to your family...'

The contempt in her voice was unmistakable. Emma stopped short, with colour flooding into her cheeks, and said, 'What is your objection to my family, Lady Osborne? I am not ashamed of them; my father was a gentleman and a scholar.'

'Perhaps. But your brother is only a surgeon's apprentice, and your sisters are well-known for running after Tom Musgrave and any other young man who will *not* have them!'

'I am very sure that my sister Elizabeth has done no such thing!' Emma cried, and then wished she had not said it.

'Your sisters Penelope and Margaret are laughed at wherever they go. Mrs Blake, no doubt, has put up with you out of kindness, but once you are in Croydon, where you belong, I do not expect to see you on my land again.'

She is mad, Emma thought, but she only said steadily, 'I will get off your land at once, Lady Osborne, but my family is quite as respectable as your own.'

She was thinking, she must not show her distress, and she must not forget the two little boys. Henry was still running about on the grass but Frank, the smaller, had come up to them and held on to her skirt, with a worried look. Lady Osborne was a whole head taller than herself and there was something alarming about her when she was glaring down, her colour high, and her eyes flashing.

'One thing more, Miss Watson. If you have designs on Mr Howard – as I think you have – let me assure you that it will be all wasted labour. I have known him longer, I know him far better than you do. He is a man of brilliant abilities, who could be a bishop within ten years, given the right friends. And his friends are *here*, in Osborne Castle; he does not want a girl with no fortune, no breeding, no—' For a moment she seemed unable to speak, then continued, 'I know that your aunt cast you off – she had her reasons, no doubt – and you have nothing to offer him. Take my word for it, Mr Howard is not for you!'

Emma replied as calmly as she could, 'Your ladyship talks of breeding. I am afraid that your own conduct seems very ill-bred to me. You are frightening the children. Come, boys, it is time we went home.'

And taking hold of Henry, who had luckily run up at just that moment, she walked very fast towards Wickstead Parsonage, clasping one boy's hand in each of hers, and scarcely conscious of the tears which were beginning to stream down her face.

## Chapter Eleven

EMMA WAS QUITE unable to account for Lady Osborne's behaviour. So unsuitable in a woman of her position, so very different from the charming manners she displayed to the rest of the world! At first it was clear to her only that she must get away, that after she had left Wickstead, which would be extremely soon, she must not come again. She told the boys, though not in very convincing tones, that there was nothing the matter with her, and in only five minutes they were back at the Parsonage.

She had dried her eyes before they got indoors and immediately little Caroline ran up, saying, 'There is a letter for you, Emma; it has just come; may I see what is in it?'

The letter was from her brother in Croydon. She immediately opened it and read:

> *'Dear Emma – I have to see Shawcross on Tuesday (1st Dec.), so will be at D. three days sooner than intended. Try to be ready for me by early afternoon, as the days are shortening.*
> *Your affect. brother, R. Watson.'*

At any other time, this news would have been most unwelcome; now, Emma was relieved, as she felt she could not bear to stay in the neighbourhood of Osborne Castle an hour longer than she absolutely must. She said, 'I am going upstairs, children', and went quickly to her room where she began to fold her dresses and gather up her few belongings, Lady Osborne's words still ringing in her ears.

What had put her into such a rage, causing her to throw off all the courtesy and restraint which, in one of her years and rank, ought to have been second nature? Only a very strong emotion could explain it, and it was not difficult to guess what that emotion was. It was Mr Howard she cared for, so much that she did not scruple to expose her feelings to a girl who was almost a stranger. Tom Musgrave had, unfortunately, been right. Despite the differences of age and wealth, Lady Osborne was passionately in love with Mr Howard.

This then was why she had felt so uncomfortable the other night. Emma tried to recall how she had behaved at the dinner party, wondering whether she had betrayed the affection she certainly did feel for Mr Howard. She hoped she had not. But Lady Osborne had evidently guessed the state of her feelings, and she grew hot with shame as she considered that others – possibly he himself – might have guessed also. She was glad he had gone away; she did not believe she could meet him again with any degree of calm.

But Mr Howard – what did *he* intend to do? Nothing had been settled between them, that was clear, or Lady Osborne would scarcely have behaved so rashly. But she remembered Tom Musgrave telling her and Margaret, 'Howard knows which side his bread is buttered.' She recoiled from the idea that a truly good man, as she knew him to be, would marry merely to get on in the world. But of course he had seen only the affable and engaging side of Lady Osborne's character. She would not have shown *him* the passionate temper which she had just shown to Emma, and she was so attractive (for her years) and had so much to offer that he might, perhaps, find her irresistible. There were her influential friends, her thirty thousand pounds; even the house in which he lived stood on the Osborne estate. As for herself, he certainly did seem to like her, but he had not long known her. He had spent years on the most intimate terms with Lord Osborne's family, and she knew almost nothing about their lives.

And even if, which now appeared impossible, he did ask her to marry him, would it not be her plain duty to refuse? Lady Osborne had made it clear that her anger would know no bounds if that happened. Mr Howard had nothing but what the Osbornes gave him. She saw his future prospects blighted, the little family, perhaps, turned out of doors; for the sake of Mrs Blake and her children it was right for her to go away and leave him to determine his own course.

As she moved about the pleasant room where she felt that she would never again stay, she reflected on the great change in her own situation since last summer. How all her troubles had dated from her uncle's death and her aunt's remarriage! If she had inherited eight or nine thousand pounds, as everyone had expected, she would then have had something solid to offer Mr Howard. She was very little consoled by the thought that had she not returned to Surrey, she would never have met him at all.

There was a gentle knock and she found Mrs Blake standing on her threshold. 'My dear Emma, what can be the matter?'

Frank piped up, 'Lady Osborne was cross, and Emma cried.'

'Go downstairs,' Mrs Blake told the child, and following Emma into her room, closed the door.

'Emma, you are distressed – Lady Osborne has said or done something to wound you – pray tell me.'

Emma said as reasonably as she could, though not quite able to suppress the signs of strong emotion, 'Mrs Blake, I must leave you soon – my brother is coming in a few hours – it matters very little what Lady Osborne said, it is enough that I am not wanted here. Please give my compliments to Mr Howard – I am sorry I shall not see him – and accept my warmest thanks for yourself, but I don't think I can ever come to Wickstead again.'

'I understand, Emma. Lady Osborne is in love with John, and cannot bear to see you with him.'

'But she is so much older!'

'Well, as to that,' Mrs Blake said smiling, 'Mr Blake was ten years older than me, and no one saw anything strange in it. If the parties are happy together, who shall judge? But I will be honest; I do not wish him to marry her. I think she is a bad woman, selfish and passionate, with little interest in her own children and no law but her own pleasure. I certainly know that she had no affection for her late husband.'

'But you are all of you so intimate!'

'I had no choice, Emma; John is compelled to be on good terms with the Osborne family, and I must follow where he leads. They are kind – in a careless way – but none of them have been brought up to think of anyone but themselves. Charles, in particular, is a great pet of theirs, but I would dread his growing up to think that he can live in the same style as the Osbornes when he will never have their income.'

'And – do you really think that your brother likes her?'

'I know only that *she* likes *him*. When we came here first, her name was linked with the Earl of – well, I must not gossip – but since his marriage, a year ago, she has spent much more of her time at the Castle, and I have watched the progress of her interest in John with growing dread. He is the kindest man alive, but, like all Englishmen, he will *not* talk about his feelings. Men are not the same as us, Emma; their passions are stronger and their insight into character, perhaps, less keen, and I can imagine that a pretty woman with charming manners might wind her way into his heart unawares. I know him to be disappointed in Lord Osborne; he has not been able to make him think seriously on any subject, but his mother was once a great beauty, you know; she is used to having men at her feet. But, Emma, if I must be honest, I have always thought he liked *you*.'

Yes, thought Emma, but there is no money on either side.

At two o'clock Robert came, impatient to be off; he said he was sure they could not get to Croydon before dark. Charles seemed inconsolable. 'There is a Christmas ball at the White

Hart,' he said, 'and I thought you were going to dance with me, Emma. Could she not stay a few weeks longer, Mr Watson? My uncle will be very sorry to find her gone.' There had been a change in the weather since morning, and rain was falling as Emma's boxes were lifted into the carriage. She looked out of the window at her friends until the last moment, convinced that she would see them no more. As the carriage began to drive past the Osbornes' long wall she gazed wearily into the drizzling rain, feeling that, in the poet's words, her grief lay onward and her joy behind.

## Chapter Twelve

THE LITTLE TOWN of Croydon stood in pleasant hilly country on the London-Brighton road, and Robert had a comfortable house, with its own walled garden, on the High Street. It was larger and better furnished than Wickstead Parsonage, but the atmosphere was inferior; Jane had been happy enough to entertain the Miss Watsons for short periods, to take them to dances and card parties in the hope of their soon finding husbands, but now that she had got three of them on her hands, with no prospect of them ever going away again, she felt that her home was no longer hers and the bad effect on her temper was marked. She had dismissed her nursemaid, and Elizabeth was now wholly responsible for the care of the two-year-old Augusta. Her youngest sister was greeted without pleasure.

'Well, Emma, you have had a fine holiday with all those grand people, but now it is time to make yourself useful, and please take this workbasket. I am not at all strong at the moment, and would really be glad of some help.'

Emma was very anxious to make herself useful, and got through a great deal of mending in the first week, but as she sat and worked, listening for much of the time to her sister's complaining, it was impossible for her to avoid the most melancholy reflections. It seemed that every home she had ever had was fated to slip away from her – the comfortable home in Shropshire which she had thought would be hers for life, then her father's house, and last Wickstead Parsonage where she had felt herself so much a part of the family. She was now fixed in

Croydon, with no expectation of things ever getting any better, and with the hope that Mr Howard might one day grow to love her, almost gone. He would be surprised, perhaps sorry, to find her absent on his return, but the chances of their meeting again must be small. Fortunately neither Robert nor Jane was at all likely to observe her low spirits.

Elizabeth now slept in the little girl's room while Emma was obliged to share Margaret's. Her sister had consented to this with a very bad grace and kept her awake half the first night talking of Tom Musgrave.

'Did you see him?' And when Emma said she had not, 'There is a ball quite soon, and I suppose I must go, but the young men in Croydon are not nearly so fine as he is. Is he not charming, Emma? So handsome, and so intimate with the Osborne family!'

Emma did not contest such wilful blindness, and made every attempt to live peaceably with the rest of the household, although Jane's ill temper made this, at times, very hard. She took a long walk towards the country whenever she could be spared, and Elizabeth sometimes joined her, with Augusta running alongside. 'I would find it very difficult to put up with,' she told her frankly, 'but for that little girl.'

One morning a note was sent home from Robert's office.

'Here is more work for me!' Jane said crossly. 'Robert writes that he has his friend Purvis with him – he is travelling back from London – and wishes to bring him home for dinner. They were at Guildford grammar school together, but we have not seen much of him lately, for his wife has long been in a decline, and she died six months ago. He has three children, I think, all less than five. Well, I am thankful to say that I always keep a good table, and I dare say he will be very glad to see us.'

As soon as the two sisters were alone Elizabeth clutched her side. 'Oh, Emma, I cannot bear it – I must stay upstairs and you must say I am unwell – and I am sure it is true, for my heart is thumping fit to burst!'

Emma got her out into the garden and they walked several times around the house together, finally sitting down at the back under the great pear tree. The fresh air seemed to revive Elizabeth but she continued to say in the most agitated tones, 'I cannot – it is impossible for me to meet him. He will wonder why he ever liked me, I am so much changed. People used to think I was a very pretty girl, but that was when I was the same age as you are now. Why, the poor man is probably still in mourning, and I could not bear him to suspect that I was trying to catch him, just because his wife is dead!'

'That is nonsense, Elizabeth,' Emma said strongly. 'Mr Purvis himself looks quite old and worn, according to Sam, and perhaps, when you have met, you will find you no longer like him. You *must* meet, or you will never be able to get him out of your head. Just be cheerful and natural as you always are, and you will both get on very well.'

'I don't think Jane knows about me and him,' Elizabeth said humbly. 'She had not met Robert, you know, when he was visiting our house, and men never gossip about these things as we do. They were trying to make a match for me with a widower of forty when I first came to Croydon, but now they think he will do better for Margaret. Jane says I am so useful to Augusta, that she is quite resigned to my being an old maid.'

'Never mind Jane! You are looking very well.' And indeed the fresh air had brought some colour into Elizabeth's cheeks. 'We will walk up to the meadows and then come back, and I will wake Gussy and take care of her while you get into your best dress.'

Elizabeth was very quiet at dinner, and hardly raised her eyes from her plate, but Emma observed that Mr Purvis looked at her with no common interest directly he came in. He was a tall stooped man with thinning hair, sad-faced and serious, and looking older than Robert although they were in fact the same age. Emma had been prepared to dislike him, but could almost forgive his treatment of her sister when she saw his confusion. There was little chance for either of them to speak as Jane talked on all the time about Penelope, and the grand marriage she was to make in two weeks.

He remained with them for several hours, took little Gussy on his knee, and Elizabeth managed a faint enquiry about his own children. He did not think there was any real weakness, he said, but they were often ill, and he was anxious to see them again. They were talking quite naturally by the time the party broke up and he was obliged to leave them to pass the night at the Star Inn.

Elizabeth sighed deeply. 'Well, it is over, and after all I am very glad to have seen him. It is like drawing a line under the whole thing in my mind.'

But the next day Emma found that she had by no means ceased to think about Purvis. He came in to pay his respects before riding back, they talked for half an hour, and when he had finally gone Elizabeth could not stop talking about him, wondering why he had called instead of hurrying home, and saying that he certainly did look much older. It was now about twelve o'clock, and they were working in the sitting room, while Augusta played on the floor with some bits of coloured material, when the little maid brought in a letter with a great seal.

'It must be for Robert – No, it is addressed to me. Well, this is the Osborne seal, but I cannot think why any of that family should write to me.'

'Do open it,' urged Elizabeth, wild with curiosity.

Emma did so, and read:

*Madam,*

*You will be surprised, I dare say, at my wanting to pay my addresses to you, but Musgrave tells me he has it from your own lips that you have no lover. This is an honourable proposal. You are the pretti-*

*est little thing I have seen in my life, and though my friends may think me mad, I am resolved to have you. I will do myself the honour of calling at your brother's house on Thursday, so you can arrange about wedding clothes and all that. I remain, madam, your most devoted,*

*Osborne*

*Don't worry about my mother as she will move into the Dower House.*

'He cannot – no, he *cannot* be serious!' Emma cried when she had finished. She read it again – and again. There could be no doubt that it really was a proposal of marriage. Elizabeth was in such a state of suspense that she had no choice but to show her the letter, but she was already angry at the young man's presumption that she would immediately fall in with his wishes, the hint that he had talked about her with his friends, and that they had spoken of her with contempt.

'He *does* mean it,' said Elizabeth in awed tones. 'Well, what a grand marriage – I never heard of such a thing! I hope I shall still see you sometimes, Emma. And his mother! Where is this dower house? it is probably twice the size of ours.'

'It is on the edge of the park, quite close enough for her to make mischief. But never mind it, Elizabeth, for I am quite resolved to have nothing to do with that family.'

At this point Mrs Robert Watson unfortunately came in, and Elizabeth at once passed on the great news that her youngest sister had received an offer – from a lord, no less – and that she supposed they would none of them be allowed to visit her when she went to live at Osborne Castle. Jane snatched the letter from her hand with the one word, 'Nonsense!' but, after she had read it, seemed perfectly stunned.

'Can he mean it? Are you sure he is not joking? Well, Emma,

this is the greatest thing that has happened to any family I know. What amazing luck! You must sit down and write to him straight away, before he changes his mind. And when he visits – I have never entertained a lord before – I must go out and get two turkeys—'

Emma, wishing very much that she had been allowed to read her letter in private, said, 'I beg you will take no trouble, Jane. I am not going to marry him.'

'Not have him! Don't talk such stuff, you foolish girl! You know you *must* marry, and there are not many penniless women, I assure you, who could expect half so great an offer. Why, everyone will be crying out on your extreme good fortune!'

'The man is stupid and coarse. He is not half so much a gentleman as – as many with a far smaller income. Pray look again at his letter, Jane; do you really think he expresses himself like a sensible man?'

'I don't believe you can turn him down, Emma,' said Elizabeth, quite shocked. 'You will never get such an opportunity again.'

'Then I must do without,' Emma said, 'for as I can neither like nor respect Lord Osborne, I am fully convinced that it would be madness to marry him. He scarcely knows me; it is just one of his odd whims.'

They continued to argue for most of the day, and the instant Robert came home, Jane flew at him with the whole story. There was then an end of all peace for Emma as her relations attacked her one after the other, all urging her not to be such a fool as to refuse this great chance. Robert, when he found that her mind was made up, grew quite angry.

'There is not any other man in question, is there? I would surely have heard of it.'

'No,' Emma said, 'there is no other man.'

'Then I cannot understand it. You won't have that pretty face for the whole of your life, Emma; in another three or four years you will be past your best, and I can tell you, miss, that there are not many young men in Croydon, let alone the House of Lords, who would dream of taking you without a sixpence. I am afraid you are being very wilful and foolish.'

'And very ungrateful,' said Jane, 'for even the food on your plate is provided by your brother and me, and it is your clear duty to make the best marriage you can. Nay, any marriage at all, even if it were to an old man like Dr Harding, and you say that this lord is quite young.'

'But,' Emma protested, 'you have not met him – he is dull and stupid—'

'That is of no consequence,' Robert said, 'you should be thinking of your family, Emma, and not only yourself. Why, you could have Margaret to stay with you at the Castle, and, I dare say, pick up a husband for her, and it would do us all a world of good if you were Lady Osborne. Sam, whom you pretend to be so fond of, could, no doubt, get a better job, and little Augusta might be received in high society when she is older. I shall take it very badly if you will not show more respect for my opinion, knowing the world as I do, and you do not.'

Emma perceived that they were all against her. Only Elizabeth, after some thought, said quietly that if Emma really disliked Lord Osborne perhaps she should not have him, as marriages between the nobility and common people were not very likely to turn out well, and the young man might, after all, be a little mad. Robert told her angrily to keep quiet, and Emma saw with how little consideration her sister was treated in their brother's house. It was a foretaste of what she herself could expect, if she did not do as he wished.

She promised, at last, that she would give it her full consideration, that she would not reply to Lord Osborne's letter until that night had passed and she had had time to reflect. She went early to her room, but was soon followed upstairs by Margaret.

'You are a great simpleton, Emma. *I* would take him, though

I have never spoken to him, but he is quite good-looking, and very rich, and I should so like to stay with you.' And Emma knew that her head was full of balls at Osborne Castle and Tom Musgrave.

There was much for her to think about, when Margaret had finally fallen asleep and she lay awake for almost half the night, listening to the clock of Croydon church chime the hours until three. Although she had been in no doubt about her feelings from the very first moment, she had now to ask, was it *right* to refuse this magnificent offer? She recalled her own words – ' we must not all expect to be individually lucky – the luck of one member of a family is luck to all.' If she accepted Lord Osborne, she would certainly be able to do something for her sisters and Sam; the small circumstance that she herself would be most unhappy was, perhaps, not important. The alternative was to live probably for the rest of her life in her brother's house, every moment made to feel her dependent position, and with much added unpleasantness in future, for she felt very sure that Jane and Robert would not soon forgive her. She listened to Margaret's snoring and thought of the thousand disadvantages of Croydon; she recalled the spacious rooms and beautiful grounds of Osborne Castle, of which she might be mistress, if she chose. She even managed a slight smile when she thought of how angry and how incredulous Lady Osborne would be. But then she recollected their last meeting; the lady's unreasonable rage about her friendship with Mr Howard, and she shuddered when she saw what she had almost agreed to do.

No, it was impossible. It would be wrong, it would be immoral to marry one man when she loved another – that other, too, whom she would be meeting all the time if she moved to Osborne Castle. There was no possibility that she could get to feel any affection for Lord Osborne with Mr Howard constantly before her eyes. And she could not pretend; he would very soon find out that she did not esteem him. The wealth, the title, the freedom from vulgar cares which would be hers could not reconcile her to the man himself. She got up perfectly resolved.

After breakfast, Robert departed for work. Jane said, '*Now*, Emma, you must write; you have left it too long already.'

Emma sat down at the writing-desk in the parlour. She thought, I am going to decide the future course of my life. After sitting quite motionless for a while, she began to write, 'Dear Lord Osborne, I regret -.'

There was a sound of hooves in the street. She dropped her pen, looked up and hurried to the window. Mr Howard on his chestnut mare had stopped outside her brother's gate.

# Chapter Thirteen

THE SENSATIONS of a young lady, when the man she has been thinking of for several days, and had little hope of meeting again, unexpectedly turns up on her very threshold, may be more easily imagined than described. Emma felt that she could scarcely breathe; she let her letter lie upon the desk and thought no more of it. He had heard, perhaps, of Lady Osborne's rudeness, and was come to apologise; or perhaps he wished to make sure that she had reached her brother's house safely. She composed herself; it was most probable that he meant – nothing at all. She hardly knew whether Elizabeth had given Margaret a hint to stay away, but, at all events, Mr Howard was ushered in a few minutes later, and she found herself absolutely alone to receive him.

She came forward, and said what was proper. He looked tired, and in worse spirits than she had ever seen him, but, as always, they had no difficulty falling into conversation.

'Mrs Blake is well? And the children?'

Yes, they were all well, but he had hardly seen them; he had been travelling a great deal between Oxford and Surrey.

'And Mr Murray? He died?'

'Yes, only a day after I arrived in Oxford. He was one of my oldest friends, a year younger than myself.' He got up, and began to pace restlessly about the room; Emma also rose. 'It was on my way back from his funeral that I quite unexpectedly met Tom Musgrave in Broad Street. I helped him back to his inn – he was the worse for drink -.'

He seemed to have some trouble continuing. Emma could only listen.

'In short,' he said abruptly, 'I heard it first from Musgrave but I know it to be true – I am aware that you have received a proposal of marriage from Lord Osborne.'

The colour rushed into Emma's cheeks; her eyes went immediately to the bit of paper, abandoned on her desk, and his followed.

'Yes. I was just going to reply.'

'Thank God,' Mr Howard said, 'then it is not settled!' He went on more composedly, 'Miss Emma, it is your decision; you may, perhaps, think me a confounded busybody, and if you turned me out of the house for meddling in your affairs I could not wonder at it, but – .'

'I would never do that,' Emma said.

'Then I beg you to hear me, before your mind is made up irrevocably. I know that, in the world's eyes, it is a brilliant match; that your friends may urge you to consent, but – Well, I must speak as I feel.' He was silent for a moment and then burst out, 'He is not fit to be in the same room with you!'

Emma was surprised at the violence of his language, and when she tried to speak, could not.

'You know,' Mr Howard said, 'that I was Lord Osborne's tutor, and that he afterwards spent three years in Oxford, although he left without a degree?'

'Yes.'

'I must tell you that during that time he got acquainted with a young woman – Miss Tate – an innkeeper's daughter. He persuaded her to leave her home. The connection went on for several years. There are two natural – two very young children.'

'I – I did not know,' Emma said.

'Of course you did not. I was not aware of it either until Musgrave told me, which he would hardly have done, I suppose, had he not been drinking. He had come to Oxford to settle matters with this poor girl – in fact, to pay her off. Lord Osborne was tired of her, he said, and wished – no, *intended* to marry you.'

'Are you sure this is true?'

'Yes, for the first thing I did was to see the young woman and her family. She seems quite broken-hearted. She told me that he had promised to marry her when he was twenty-five and should have the power to do as he wished. Of course he had no such intention. I then rode back to Wickstead and went up to the Castle to see him.'

'What does his mother think?' asked Emma, suddenly alarmed.

'I have not asked her. I spoke only to Lord Osborne him-self. He – well, Miss Emma, I need not repeat the whole of our conversation. I told him that, given the length of the con-nection, I really thought he should marry her, and that whatever his friends or family might say, his first duty was towards the children he had brought into the world. He laughed, and said they would do much better in their own rank of life, and that I ought to congratulate him for throwing off his mistress, and marrying a virtuous young woman – yourself. Neither he nor Musgrave seemed to have a doubt that you *would* marry him.'

'I—'

'So I told him that if he did not inform you, I would. He told me to go to the devil. He also said that he was expecting to receive your acceptance at any moment. We parted on thor-oughly bad terms and... well, Emma – Miss Watson – I have ridden here on purpose to see you. You know the full story now, and it is your choice.'

His restless pacings around the small room had brought him to within a foot of her; Emma realised that they were standing unwontedly close together, that her head was almost brushing his sleeve. They both started back and at the same moment she saw Jane opening the garden gate, and realised that they would not much longer be left alone. She forced herself to appear calm, and said, walking to her desk:

'You should not have believed him, Mr Howard; I have never promised. Look' – she put the unfinished letter into his hand – 'before you came, I had already decided to refuse Lord Osborne.'

His face brightened, and he seemed about to speak, but before he could say a word Jane bustled in, welcoming him effusively and saying that she remembered him very well. She talked for so long, indeed, that Emma was almost breathing easily once more before she heard Jane invite him to stay to dinner, as her husband would be glad to meet him.

'That is very kind, Mrs Watson,' Mr Howard said, 'but I fear I must leave almost at once; I promised my sister to be back by nightfall and my parish has been sadly neglected in the last week. Pray give my compliments to all your family. We shall meet again, Miss Emma.'

A quick press of the hand, and he was gone; Emma watched Jane accompany him to the door and realised that he had silently thrust her letter into his pocket and taken it away with him. She leaned against the wall, almost too much moved to think, dreading only that Jane would begin to ask questions. But her sister was called away by the cook, and she was left in peace. She immediately sat down and wrote a decided refusal to Lord Osborne, took it to the post office, and left it.

## Chapter Fourteen

'WELL, EMMA,' said Mrs Robert Watson, the moment her sister walked back in, 'now I see why you could not be persuaded to marry the lord. You sly creature; I suppose you fixed it up when you were staying at Wickstead. He is a fine figure of a man, my dear; I congratulate you with all my heart. What is money when one is in love? and, after all, I suppose he has enough for the two of you to live on.'

'Indeed, Jane,' Emma said earnestly, 'I am not engaged to Mr Howard.'

'No, no, I came in at just the wrong moment, didn't I? but he's sure to be back. Margaret will be wild with jealousy because she is older than you, but if she wants to find a husband of her own she will just have to behave more pleasantly. I am getting really tired of her peevish ways.'

The truth was that Jane had taken an immediate liking to Mr Howard, whose good appearance, pleasant manners to herself and obvious interest in Emma had convinced her of his being a very suitable person to take that young woman off her hands. Her sisters, too, were perfectly convinced that Mr Howard was in love with her, and that if they were not yet engaged, it must soon happen. Robert was less sanguine when Jane told him at dinner of the day's events.

'Hah, you women see a love story everywhere, and I shall always say it was very foolish of Emma to turn down such a fine offer. Howard is a very good sort of man; I have seen him once or twice, but when all is said, he is only a parson.'

'You have not seen him as I have, Robert,' said his wife. 'I do like a man who is tall, and he has the most attractive dark eyes; I declare that I should be very much taken with him, if I was not a married woman, my dear. The only thing I do not quite like, is that he has no powder in his hair, but no doubt Emma can persuade him to smarten himself up, once they are married.'

Robert was unimpressed. 'Just because Emma has a fancy for Howard, it is sheer folly to snub a man of ten times his consequence. He has not yet made her an offer, has he? No, I thought not. Then she may very well end up with no husband at all, and will be sorry she did not take the lord, who could have done so much for our family. Well, at least Penelope's wedding is next week, and then there will be only three girls left. What man would choose to have sisters?'

All this was not very pleasant for Emma, but she continued to say, quietly but firmly, that Mr Howard had called merely to see that she had reached Croydon safely, and to pay his respects to her family. She had decided not to repeat what he had told her about Lord Osborne. The secret was not hers, and, although it had distressed, it had not deeply shocked her, as she had never had a high opinion of the young man in any case. If Robert *had* known, she feared that he would have told her not to mind.

But it was hard to keep as cool as she wished, when both Jane, and Elizabeth, and her own heart told her it was very likely that Mr Howard wanted to pay his addresses to her. She remembered his strong grasp of her hand, his hurried words, 'We shall meet again, Miss Emma.' She had not forgotten Lady Osborne's behaviour, and had determined that if he *did* speak, she must at once tell him of that lady's implacable hostility. But the more she thought, the more she was convinced that the two families could not go on in the same parish; the bitter disagreement he had had with Lord Osborne must make that impossible. Yet it might not be in his power to give up the living of

Wickstead; he had not only himself to think of, and she did not know what other possibilities were open to him. She wore herself out thinking of what he might do, and sometimes felt he would have no choice but to grow grey in an Oxford college, paying all he had to support his sister and her children.

Two days passed uneventfully, and on the third, Robert, with very black looks, had just left for his office when a smart curricle drew up outside the house, and out leapt Tom Musgrave, his hair freshly powdered, his whole person breathing an assurance of being welcome wherever he went. This time Jane was at home and received him graciously. Margaret seemed almost beside herself with joy, and the young man greeted them with no signs of recalling, or being embarrassed by, the condition he had been in when they last saw him. After talking for a short while he turned to Jane and said most politely, 'May I, madam, have the favour of a few minutes' conversation with Miss Emma Watson?'

Jane consented in a great flutter, and the three older ladies left the room; Emma perceived that they thought he was come to make her an offer, and that Margaret, for one, was very much displeased. For herself she was not greatly troubled. She had almost fainted the other day, when she found herself alone with Mr Howard, but she thought that she could manage Tom Musgrave very well. She sat down once more, and asked him to state his business.

Tom hummed and hawed. 'Well, Miss Emma, I expect you know what I am come to say?'

'Indeed I don't, sir.'

'The truth is, then, that Lord Osborne has received your note, turning down his offer. He is very much surprised, and so were all of them at the Castle. With all due respect to your family, they couldn't think why a girl without any fortune should say no to a peer of the realm. It's a very good offer, you know; there are plenty of ladies in London who are wild to get him.'

'I should be sorry to cause pain to anyone,' said Emma, 'but I feel sure his lordship will soon be consoled by one of these London ladies you mention; I am convinced that he and I would not suit.'

'But what's the problem, Miss Emma? Osborne fancied that you might be afraid of his mother, but he believes he has already said something about that – she'll be packed off to the Dower House, just as soon as you two are married.'

'His mother has nothing to do with me, Mr Musgrave.'

'Ah, but that's not quite true, because, you see, I know that you and she had a great argument.' Emma was amazed, and could say nothing. 'She's all sugar and spice, that lady, when things are going her way, but in private she has the devil of a temper. I've seen her once or twice, when she was offended with her daughter or the servants, and – whew! Now, you may think you were unobserved, but there are a great many windows on the east front, and the housekeeper saw her walk towards you, and stop, and she could tell from her Ladyship's gestures that there was a quarrel, although she could not of course hear what was said. And I find that one of the gardeners heard two women raising their voices on the same day.'

'I did *not* raise my voice!' Emma said.

'Of course not,' Tom said soothingly, 'but I don't blame you for being frightened; she's a formidable lady. I mention it just to prove to you, that I know most of what goes on in that house. Well, Osborne and I put our heads together, and of course we concluded she was warning you off him. She don't seem to realise, her son is a grown man. I understand that you left Wickstead that very same day, to be out of her sight.'

'I left because my brother called for me, and really, Mr Musgrave—'

'But, Miss Emma, I am come to tell you, the old lady will be no problem at all, because she is going much further away than the Dower House. The truth is, everything is settled between her and Howard. I told you that she had a fancy for him, did I not? They will marry quite quietly in the next few weeks to avoid any unpleasantness from her relations, and then she will take him to Wimpole Street and introduce him to some grand people in London, so she can get him a stall, or a see. He'll be a bishop, she says, by the year 'twelve at latest. I should not much care for that sort of job myself,' Tom said honestly, 'but every man to his taste. Well, to sum up, you need not see her more than once or twice a year, and by that time you will be Lady Osborne, not she, so you may snub her to your heart's content.'

'Are you sure that it is settled?'

'Yes, certain. I have already met the man who is to get the living, for he dined at the Castle on Wednesday. The only thing I don't yet know is what is to happen to Howard's sister and her children, but the boys, I suppose, will go to school, and Mrs Blake will probably get a little house somewhere, as her Ladyship won't want to have her living *en famille*. So now, my dear Miss Emma, what have you to say to my friend's proposal?'

In all her agony of mind, Emma had time to feel a quick flash of contempt both for Lord Osborne, too idle to press his own suit, and for Tom, who, it seemed, was prepared to carry out any mean office to ingratiate himself with the richer man. She stood up.

'I can say only what I said before, sir, and I have nothing to add. Pray excuse me.'

She was trying to get at the door, but Tom Musgrave half blocked it.

'But... I say, Miss Emma, you never heard about the love-children, did you? Because no sensible girl—'

Emma got past him and attained her room, which fortunately was not occupied by Margaret, where she closed the door and gave way to an agony of tears.

## Chapter Fifteen

EMMA'S PAIN WAS now much greater than on the occasion in the park when Lady Osborne had abused her. Then, it had merely been a threat that she might marry Mr Howard; now, it was settled. She wished to, but she could not doubt that Tom Musgrave, with his intimate knowledge of the Castle family, knew of what he spoke.

But why should Mr Howard, with his excellent qualities and clear understanding, unite himself to such a woman? Alas, she reminded herself again, he knew only half of Lady Osborne's character. Her charming manners (to those she wished to please), her beauty which had everything but the bloom of youth, might prevail on him as they had on so many other men. Moreover, he had not only his own wishes to consult; he must also consider the welfare of Mrs Blake and her children, and who knew but such a marriage might seem to him the right, the prudent thing to do?

It was only three days since he had spoken to her, and from his words and gestures on that occasion she was almost sure – no, *quite* sure that he liked her. But he might like her, might, in other circumstances, have wished to marry her, yet resolve that any nearer connection would be unwise. He had wanted to save her from a life with Lord Osborne that certainly would have been most unhappy, but would carefully guard himself against ever seeing her again. Indeed, if she *had* married Lady Osborne's son, he and she must have been continually thrown together, and that prospect was not to be borne.

She heard someone coming up the stairs, and shrank; she did not want to meet any of the family, in her misery. But it was only Elizabeth. 'My dear Emma,' she said breathlessly, 'don't come down yet; Jane is in a rage, because she had quite made up her mind that Mr Howard was to marry you and not her Ladyship.'

'How does she know?' Emma asked dully.

'Well, you know, if you are in the front passage, you can hear every word that is said in the parlour, and Jane stood herself there as soon as you had shut the door and heard it all. It was very wrong of her, but this is her house, and what could I do? You see, she had great hopes, first that Mr Howard was come to propose for you, and then that it was Tom Musgrave, and now it seems you are not going to marry anybody.'

'No, Eliza, I don't think I am.'

'You poor girl,' Elizabeth said, warmly embracing her sister. 'I hope it is not true, for I have come to like Mr Howard very much, but he must be quite, quite mad if he prefers Lady Osborne to you. What a way for a woman of fifty to carry on! It would be much more fitting to devote herself to good works, at her time of life.'

Emma could not imagine Lady Osborne devoting herself to good works at any time of her life, but she attempted to smile.

'And it seems you will not have the lord either,' said Elizabeth, taking out her handkerchief. 'Well, perhaps it is for the best; I am sure she would have given you a dreadful time as your mother-in-law. But, Emma, I just came up to say you must be careful, because Jane will be here at any moment. She would have been with you as soon as Tom Musgrave left, but Gussy happened to fall down and hurt her leg, and she is still howling.'

And indeed, Emma could now hear the sound of a child crying, of which she had been quite unaware.

She dried her eyes, and Jane came up soon afterwards in a towering rage. 'Well, miss, I hope you know what you are doing, because I can make no sense of it. All these young men writing and coming to the house, and still no engagement! I don't know who you think is going to have you, unless it is one of the royal dukes, for it seems you are too vain to take anyone lower. Is it because of the natural children? Oh, yes, Mr Musgrave has informed me of that. Let me tell you, that if Lord Osborne had *four* of them instead of two, that would not be your affair; it is your duty to stop living off your brother and me, and marry as well as you can. And – well, now who in the world is that? I am sick and tired of all these visitors!'

They looked out of the window and saw a carriage, quite unknown to them, stop outside, and a moment later Penelope with a servant got out of it. Jane ran down to meet them, and Emma and Elizabeth watched in amazement as boxes were carried to the door, and the coachman prepared to drive away. Their sister did not look like a lady about to be married. She had a great deal of luggage, and appeared to be in much distress. Elizabeth exclaimed, 'Gracious me, Emma, I wonder if Dr Harding has broke it off? I was always afraid that he might.'

They went downstairs and found Penelope in the hall, surrounded by her boxes and weeping copiously. Margaret was standing by but made no attempt to comfort her.

'Where is Dr Harding?' Jane asked blankly.

'Dr Harding is *dead*! A fit of asthma carried him off on Tuesday after a short struggle. I shall never recover from this. You must take me in, Jane; this is the only home I have!' And she flung herself, still weeping, into the arms of her dismayed sister-in-law.

Jane called for tea, and Elizabeth helped her into the parlour, made her lie on the sofa and gave her some lavender drops. Emma had never admired her eldest sister so much as now, when she saw how tenderly she attended Penelope, but for whom, perhaps, she herself could have been a married woman years ago. The past seemed quite forgotten as she said with concern, 'Hush, hush, my dear Penny – I am sure you are in the deepest grief but you will make yourself ill if you cry so.' But Penelope continued crying, so loudly that she frightened little Augusta, and complaining that no one else had ever had her extreme bad luck.

'If it had only happened one week later! Then I should have been Mrs Harding and could have turned that cat, Louisa Monks, out of the house! Now she will get everything, and instead of being sorry for me she is clamouring for some jewels which Dr Harding gave me, and which she says belong to her, but I am determined she shall not have them.'

'I don't think you can do that, Pen,' said Robert, who had come home while this was going on and was standing around with a very long face. 'If Dr Harding bought them for you, they are your own, but if they are her mother's jewels I am afraid that she has a right to them.'

'It is only an emerald ring,' said Penelope, weeping into her cup of tea, 'and two or three gold necklaces of not much value. Who could grudge them to me after all I have suffered? She is a wicked woman, you know, Robert. She never made me feel welcome in the house, or wanted her old father to have any happiness, and I hoped she might be packed off to Bath once we were safely married. To think that it should all end like this!'

'What I want to know,' said Jane, who had been showing signs of impatience, 'is where must Penelope be put to sleep? Elizabeth and Gussy are in one bedroom, and Emma and Margaret in another, and there is nothing left but the garrets. I think we shall just have to move in another bed, and the three of them must get on as best they can. I always told you, Robert, that this house was too small.'

'There is no space for the three of us in one room!' cried Margaret.

Emma began to fear, that although just now Penelope was the centre of attention, the family could only become more unhappy, and she herself would not escape blame in the days and weeks to come.

## Chapter Sixteen

EMMA HAD BEEN RIGHT in thinking that Jane would be very angry with her for refusing Lord Osborne, since she now had no other prospect. The next day, when her cousin, Mrs Pratt, a narrow-minded woman very like herself, called, she complained in her presence that two of her husband's sisters had been on the point of getting married, and after all nothing had come of it.

'I cannot blame Penelope,' she said, 'for it was not her fault that Dr Harding died when he did, but Emma had two chances with Lord Osborne, and without even bothering to ask my advice, she refused! She did indeed, cousin. It is very hard to have all four of them living here, taking away from little Gussy's portion, and between ourselves I expect to have another one in the summer, although I had hoped it would not be quite so soon. And now of course they all want me to take them to parties, even though they are in mourning, but I am in a very delicate state, and why should I take any trouble for Emma, when she won't take any for herself?'

Mrs Pratt said what was proper, but Emma perceived that she did not believe Jane, for it was not credible that a lord could really wish to marry one of their family, or that he could be refused, if he did. A lord! no, no, she could imagine her telling her husband, Jane was making it up to give herself importance.

It was a relief, however, that she heard no more from Lord Osborne, who seemed at last to have accepted her decision. She thought much of Mr Howard, and of the happy days she had spent at Wickstead, where there was no selfish discontent, no small-minded quarrelling such as she had constantly to endure in Croydon. Her nights were made miserable by the arguments between Penelope and Margaret, in the narrow bedroom which the three girls shared. 'I don't see why Penelope should get all the sympathy,' Margaret complained whenever she and her youngest sister were alone together. 'Everybody knows that she did not like Dr Harding, and indeed no one could, for he was a very nasty old man.'

As the days went by, Emma in her misery began to think that she might leave her brother's house and get some sort of post, even teaching in a school, as she had once mentioned to Elizabeth. She liked children, and, whatever the evils of life as a governess, she sometimes thought that they could hardly be worse than life in what was now her home. All four sisters were aware that Jane resented their presence, although Elizabeth spent most of every day and night looking after little Augusta. Her expected confinement had made her cross and nervous, and they were never quite safe from her assaults. Robert was more reasonable, but nevertheless had made it clear to Emma that he was very much displeased.

Christmas was approaching, and Jane reluctantly exerted herself to take Emma and Margaret to some quiet parties. Emma found two or three young men to talk with, but none, to her mind, could stand comparison with Mr Howard. Alas, it was not so easy to do as she knew she should and dismiss him from her thoughts.

Sam talked of getting over for Christmas and Boxing Day. Emma thought she might consult him on her future; he was a man, and knew the world, and might be able to advise her about some respectable employment.

She was also hoping to hear from Wickstead, for she could settle to nothing until she knew if Mr Howard was married. *Then*, she hoped, she could resolve to forget him, but meanwhile she kept herself busy with preparations for Christmas and attempted to placate Jane by keeping out of her way. At last a letter arrived. She tore it open, but it was not the news she dreaded.

Mrs Blake apologised for not having written sooner, but all the children had been ill with colds and she had not had a moment to spare. 'I am sure you have done the right thing in refusing Lord Osborne,' she added; 'you never could have been happy with such a man. Even if his private character had been all that it ought to be, he is still far too heavy and lumpish for you. I don't think he and John can ever be friends again, for they had a great argument when he came back from Croydon, and he will never believe that the decision was your own. He now spends almost every day shooting. I think that we may not remain at Wickstead much longer – but when I know where I am to go I will tell you more – wherever, I hope it will not be long before we meet again, my dear Emma. Charles is calling me from his bed and I must run!'

Leaving Wickstead! – what could this mean? Emma knew not what to think. She could easily believe, that it would be unpleasant for Mr Howard and Lord Osborne to have any further dealings with one another, and if Lady Osborne really intended to marry him that would not mend matters, for her son and daughter could only think it a most unsuitable and degrading connection. She puzzled over the letter for some time, but in the end wrote back, thanking her friend again for her hospitality, and sending her particular love to little Charles.

Two days before Christmas Eve, Elizabeth had just entered from the street holding Augusta's hand to find Jane complaining, as usual, to all who would listen, that it was very hard, in her present state of health, to have to take her husband's sisters everywhere, because they could none of them pick up a husband.

'My dear Jane,' Robert said, 'you knew very well when you married me that I had four sisters. It is my duty to provide for them and I will do so, although Emma has behaved like a fool, as you say. We can throw a party or two once we are out of mourning, and, who knows, if we get a regiment quartered at Croydon they might meet some officers – .'

'You will not have to provide for me much longer, Robert,' Elizabeth said, in a shaking voice. 'Mr Purvis has asked me to marry him. It happened just now, when we were walking down the High Street in full view of everybody, and he is waiting in the hall, until I have broke it to you. I shall be very sorry to leave Gussy, but he has three children, you know, who ought to have a mother's care. I am going over to meet them next Saturday, and then we are to be married, just as soon as they can call the banns.'

The surprise and pleasure of Mr and Mrs Watson at this wholly unexpected piece of news were worth seeing. Jane indeed felt that she would have preferred to get rid of Penelope, since Elizabeth was devoted to her child, and put up with her own bad temper more quietly than the younger girls, but even before she had finished congratulating her, she had settled with herself that Emma should be the one to have the future charge of Augusta. Penelope gave a low moan, and ran out of the room before Purvis could be brought in. He came, and expressed himself so really delighted, and so sensible of Elizabeth's merits, that there could be very little doubt of their happiness. Emma indeed felt that this almost middle-aged pair had a far better chance of contentment than many who had married in the first flush of youth and romance. The wedding was to be in the New Year, after which Elizabeth would move into his ramshackle vicarage and begin to be acquainted with his children.

The whole family – but for Penelope, who sent word that she had a headache – dined together with the happiest feelings before Purvis was obliged to leave. Later Emma slipped into Elizabeth's room, and while Augusta slept deeply in her cot, talked it over.

'I did not know that you had ever seen him, after that first time.'

'He rode over twice,' Elizabeth said, 'and accidentally met me when I was out with Gussy. The first time I asked him to come in, but he would not, and the second I was afraid to ask, because by then Penelope was back at home. So we went to the churchyard where it is quiet, and sat among the stones and talked. It is so hard, Emma, having your every movement watched.' Emma could only agree. 'It is very awkward, but perhaps I shall not see much of Penny, because Alford is quite a remote place, and I shall be extremely busy with all those children. They are Edward, William and little Anne. The eldest is not quite five, and I hope they will get to like me. I am sure I shall do my best to be a good mother to them.'

'*I* am sure,' said Emma warmly, 'that he and they are very lucky to get you.'

'It is not really so sudden, because we were very much attached to each other when we were younger. He was not very happy with his wife, Emma. He will not say so, but I am certain of it, for he has said again and again that he made a great mistake in letting me go. Do you remember me saying once that I would take any good-humoured man, even though he were not Purvis? How thankful I am, now, that I waited all these years! Although to be out of *this* house,' said Elizabeth, 'even though it were not with him, will be a blessing.'

Emma fervently, though silently, concurred.

'It is only you, Emma, and little Gussy, that I shall regret. You must often come and stay with us. I would gladly offer a home to you or Margaret, but perhaps she would not like that much, as there are hardly any suitable young men at Alford.'

'No, Elizabeth, I feel sure she would *not* like it, and I don't think newly-married people should have anyone else living with them if it can be avoided. Perhaps Jane's temper will improve when there are only three of us in the house instead of four.'

But in her heart Emma did not think that probable, and felt that her situation could only get worse, when the most deserving of her sisters was gone. Elizabeth buried in a small village, where she could only hope to see her once or twice a year!

## Chapter Seventeen

THE FEW REMAINING days before Christmas were taken up with the jollities of the season and with preparations for Elizabeth's marriage. Robert worked himself up into a fit of generosity and gave her a present of five pounds for wedding-clothes. He also drove her over to Alford to meet Purvis and his children, a visit from which she returned very happy. Penelope sulked, and quarrelled a great deal with Margaret and Jane. She had not really wanted Purvis for herself, but was angry that her sister should get him, after what had passed. She told everyone that 'he had gone off very much, and was almost bald.'

The goose, the mince pies, and the cakes were all prepared on Christmas Eve, by which time there was a little snow, but this seemed unlikely to lie long or to make the roads impassable. In the morning, a letter came for Emma. She was always nervous of the post, lest it should contain news of Mr Howard, but on this occasion her feelings changed to delight, when she perceived the familiar and well-loved hand of her Aunt Turner. It had been several weeks since she had heard from her, and her surprise was the greater, when she saw that it was written from an address in Hampstead:

*My dear niece,*

*You will be surprised to see from this that I am back in England, but I have only just crossed the Irish channel, in more distress of mind than I can describe. Since we last met, you have lost your dear*

*father, and I – but I will not write more, in a letter which anybody*
*might see.  It is enough to say, that Captain O'Brien and myself*
*have parted; there have been irreconcilable differences, and (on his*
*side) great cruelty.  My dear Emma, I don't know if you can ever*
*forgive me for abandoning you, but I am writing to beg you to come*
*here as soon after Christmas as you can; I shall be delighted to*
*receive you for as long as you want it.  I have taken a little cottage*
*near Hampstead Heath, and am known to my neighbours as Mrs*
*Turner, for I don't think I could ever again live in Shropshire, after*
*what has passed.*

*S. O'Brien*

Emma immediately resolved to go to her as soon as she could,
but she was first obliged to show the letter to Robert, who read
it three times in silent astonishment.

'Well, you must certainly go to Hampstead and find out what
is going on, but I don't know whether her husband will permit
her to live away from him.  He has the right to all her money,
you know.  I wonder if they really have parted for good or if it
is just a tiff.  What sort of a man is he, Emma?'

'He is very affable,' Emma replied, 'very pleasant on a first
meeting, but I am afraid that my aunt has been sadly deceived in
him.  Certainly as soon as they were married he turned against
me, and insisted that I should at once be sent back to our father.'

'He married her for her money, I suppose?'

'I am not sure that it was only that.  She is a fine-looking
woman for her age, and has an amiable temper, but I believe, if
there had been *no* money, he probably would not have married
her.  Robert, I am most anxious to see her.  If she is able to
offer me a home, I shall take it, for there are already too many
of us, as you know, in your house.'

Robert considered it.  'Sam or I shall take you.  You must
not expect to be an heiress any longer, Emma, for as I said, the

husband gets all, but if he were to die, or if she has been able to salvage any of her fortune, it could be quite a good thing for you.'

Although they went to bed very late, Sam was still later, and Emma did not see him until she came down to breakfast on Christmas Day. He met her with the happiest face and his arms full of presents, saying, 'Congratulate me, Emma; I am a made man; old Curtis has taken me into partnership and I shall soon be able to afford to move into my own house.'

The family were all delighted at his good fortune.

'I don't think anybody has worked as hard as I have over the last twelve months,' said Sam, 'but the old boy has had some palpitations with his heart, and the practice is getting too much for him.' And he gave them some further details as he sat down to his ham and eggs with great relish.

'Dear Sam,' cried Elizabeth, 'I don't think anybody could deserve it more than you do.'

'And when you get your own house, are you going to be married, Sam?' Margaret enquired eagerly. 'I dare say I could come and keep house for you, if you were not, but what does Mary Edwards say?'

He looked conscious, and said that nothing was settled, but it was obvious from his sparkling eyes that the affair was not going too badly. Emma in sympathy turned the conversation on to something else. Sam said that if he had known who Purvis was, he should have looked at him closer, and that he would certainly ride over for Elizabeth's wedding, which was fixed for the second week in January.

All this talk of marriage made Penelope very unhappy, and she withdrew straight after breakfast. She condescended to appear again at church, dressed in deep mourning, and was afterwards seen to exchange words with various neighbours and accept their condolences with eyes modestly cast down.

Mrs O' Brien's letter was then talked over, and Sam readily agreed to drive Emma to Hampstead the following day.

'It may turn out well,' said Robert, 'but you must bring her back, if it is not a suitable place for her.'

Emma could not imagine a more suitable place than with her aunt, if the Captain really meant to keep away from them, and she and Sam set out at first light on Boxing Day. There was snow on the distant hills, but the roads were clear, and as they jogged along, Sam told her what had been happening.

'I always liked Mary, as you know, Emma, but Mr and Mrs Edwards were against me, and for a long time I thought it was almost hopeless. But the truth is that her mother disliked Captain Hunter, and thought after all that it would be better to have her settled in Guildford than roaming about with the regiment, given the way my fortunes have improved. So we have got this far, that if I continue to do well, we may be married in about a year. It has taken me some time to convince the old people I am not a fortune-hunter. I never cared about her ten thousand pounds; I should still have wanted to marry her if she had been penniless, but it will certainly make things easier if we have enough to live on. Then, perhaps, I can do something for you girls. Would you like to live in Guildford, Emma? There will be parties and all that. You like Mary, do you not?'

'Very much,' Emma said sincerely. She was not sure that she could quite forgive Mary Edwards, who had certainly for a time overlooked Sam's real worth for the glamour of a red coat, but, since all was settled, she would hope for the best. And she consoled herself that, whether or not the marriage came off, Sam's prospects now looked much better than they had only a few weeks before.

They crossed London Bridge, and in late morning found themselves in the delightful village of Hampstead, with its sloping streets, pure air, and great expanse of heath offering remarkable views over London. Soon they arrived at a small cottage in Flask Walk, and Emma found herself embraced by her aunt, whom she had not seen for three months.

## Chapter Eighteen

Mrs O'Brien was a remarkably good-looking woman for her years, with a strong resemblance to Emma's late mother, and possessing a generous and romantic temperament that made her universally loved, but, Emma was sure, had caused her to suffer greatly since they had last met. The brother and sister were welcomed with delight.

'Dearest Emma, I did not dare expect you quite so soon. And this is little Sam! Why, you are almost six feet tall! I am looking forward to getting better acquainted with all my nephews and nieces, now that I am settled so near.'

Tea was brought, and Mrs O'Brien explained that the cottage had but one spare bedroom, but that should be Emma's for as long as she wished. Her enthusiasm for having her niece to live with her again seemed so great that Sam was obliged to say, 'I have to return tonight, ma'am, but, pray don't be offended, I wouldn't wish to leave my sister here, if her presence was at all disagreeable to Captain O'Brien.'

'You need have no fears of *that*,' his aunt said warmly. 'Mr O'Brien is now on his way to India, and, I hope and believe, will never trouble me again. No, Emma is welcome to share my home, until she leaves it for one of her own, and I shall be happy to entertain you and your other sisters whenever you are near me. And now let us walk out before dinner, so that I may show you a little of Hampstead.'

They assented, and wandered about for more than an hour admiring all they saw; the mineral springs, Mr Romney's studio, now deserted, the children flying kites upon the heath were all noticed and praised. At length they returned to the cottage for a leisurely dinner; Mrs O'Brien said much about the pleasures of Hampstead, where she had now been living for a week, but very little about the circumstances which had caused her to settle, with such suddenness, in a neighbourhood where she was quite unknown. Sam left as soon as they had got up from table, for he had to go back to Croydon and ride to Guildford the next morning.

'And I expect to see you both at Elizabeth's wedding,' were his parting words. 'That will not be very long, and I am glad to leave you in such good hands, Emma.'

'Dear Eliza!' sighed Mrs O'Brien as they waved him off. 'I remember her as a very pretty girl, but she must now be almost thirty. Do you think the man will be kind to her, Emma?'

'I really believe so, aunt.'

'That is a relief. And Mr Purvis has been known to your family for a long time, you say? I would caution any young woman against marrying a man who is a total stranger, of whom she knows only that he has an attractive person and smooth, plausible manners. Emma, I have used you most unjustly!'

It was followed by a burst of tears.

'My dear aunt,' Emma cried, 'you have nothing to reproach yourself with; you were the sufferer, not I, and at least my leaving you has enabled me to grow acquainted once more with my brothers and sisters.' As she spoke, she reflected that only two of the five had proved real friends to her, but it was true that she could never regret having come back into Surrey. 'I beg that you will never mention it again.'

By degrees, Mrs O'Brien grew calmer, and, after the candles had been lit in the small sitting-room, told her story.

'I blame myself very greatly for all that took place. Your uncle and I had a most happy marriage, as you know, but during the years when he was so ill, the quiet life in the country depressed me and I longed for a change. I think I was a little mad, Emma. Nothing else could have induced me to reject a child, whom I had known and loved for fourteen years, for a man I had known barely four weeks. Even so, I had no idea of leaving you – I fully intended to keep you with us, and it was a great shock when he insisted you should go back to your father. But by that time we were married – I had little choice – and he persuaded me he was so much in love that he could not bear to have a third person present.'

Emma pressed her hand in sympathy.

'Well – I missed you very much when we arrived in Ireland. It is a beautiful country, and I should have liked to show you Dublin, where we spent a few tolerably happy weeks. But pretty soon I began to regret what I had done; I worried about how you were getting on, and I think I reproached him, for forcing you to leave me.'

'Dear aunt, I never wanted to make trouble for you!'

'Oh, my dear, he was quite capable of making trouble for himself! Such a set of men as his friends were! Sitting up all night, and drinking themselves under the table, and losing enormous quantities of money at cards! Our life soon became hideous; it was impossible to get any peace in my own home, for those dreadful men hardly ever went away. I soon discovered that he was deep in debt, and that was the reason he had married me. Our quarrels grew more frequent and bitter, until at last he moved into his mistress's house. He had known this woman, on and off, for years, and frankly said that he preferred her society to mine. After such a great and public insult, I believed I owed him nothing more, but I had not yet decided what to do, when his regiment was ordered to India.'

'And he is halfway there now?'

'Yes. I told him that I was not going with him; if the climate had not killed me, I am sure that his unkindness would have done so.' Mrs O'Brien wiped her eyes. 'He is not altogether a bad man, my dear. He consented that I should return to England, with what I could retrieve from your poor uncle's fortune – and I have some jewels, besides, that he knows nothing about. However, he believes me to be at our house in Shropshire, and I am determined never to return *there*; I could not face the smiles and sneers of my old neighbours – who all thought I was mad to marry him, in any case.'

Emma remembered what had been said at the time, and agreed.

'So in this place I am Mrs Turner, the widow of a Shropshire gentleman. It is so far away from my former connections that no one is likely to discover me, and we have enough to live on in comfort, though not luxury. But, Emma, I shall not be able to give you more than a thousand pounds; the fortune that should have been yours is almost frittered away. When you marry, my child, let it be a man that your reason approves – do not throw yourself away in a fit of passion. I am far, *far* happier as a single woman than if Mr O'Brien and I had continued together.'

Emma had learned caution in the last few months, and she did not yet say anything of Mr Howard, although she believed that her aunt would certainly approve of him. His good qualities were known to everyone – his family affection, his unswerving principle – the only drawback was that, for all she knew, he might now be the husband of Lady Osborne.

## Chapter Nineteen

FOR THE NEXT WEEK Emma continued to live happily with her aunt, finding the cottage in Flask Walk far more congenial than the far more spacious home she had left in Croydon. Besides the delightful situation, there was much going on in Hampstead – musical evenings, a library, a constant stream of visitors to take the waters. Mrs O'Brien was already on excellent terms with her neighbours, and aunt and niece were invited to some cheerful parties for the New Year. She had also fixed up a little art room, and was talking of making an income, like Miss Kaufmann, by painting portraits. Her lively, gregarious temper was not made for misery. She would soon have almost forgotten that ill-judged marriage which might have ruined another woman's whole happiness, and if the Captain did not return, as she trusted he would not, Emma felt that they might do very well.

She still thought constantly of Mr Howard, and was greatly surprised when her letter to Mrs Blake was sent back, with an intimation that the family was no longer at Wickstead. She wondered much, but dreaded to ask, where they had all gone; with so many acquaintances left in Surrey, she would surely discover soon enough what was happening.

I must be firm, she said to herself. When I *know* that he is married, or when so much time has passed as to make it certain he has no wish to see me again, perhaps I will find the strength to banish him from my mind and heart.

They were now looking forward to Elizabeth's wedding, which was to take place on the fourteenth of January. Mrs O'Brien had always wished to know her sister's children better, and, but for living at such a distance, would certainly have seen more of them; now, she was hoping with her usual optimism that all her nieces would resemble Emma.

In the early days of the year there was a heavy snowfall. The streets were soon cleared, but it continued very cold. On the morning of 4th January, Emma struggled into her pattens after breakfast and went out for her usual long walk on the heath. Her aunt was eagerly devouring a new novel, and would not join her. Only a few other people were to be seen, and she struck out along the snowy paths with a sense of delightful liberty. Here she could roam as she wished, with no Lady Osborne to order her off her land. She walked briskly for more than a mile, past the frozen ponds and into sight of Kenwood House, then turned back, cheeks glowing from the exercise, and was just about to cross Heath Road when she heard a familiar voice call her name.

'Emma! We have been looking everywhere for you!' And little Charles Blake leapt off his horse, ran across the road and flung his arms around her.

Emma returned his embrace, really delighted to see her little friend after four weeks' absence, and a moment afterwards looked up with a deep blush and became aware of his uncle's tall figure standing behind him.

'We have ridden over from Highgate,' he said, 'not far away. I am happy to see you looking so well, Miss Emma. Your aunt told us that we might find you on the heath.'

'She seems a very nice lady,' added Charles, 'and we are all going back to her house to drink chocolate.'

Emma noticed that his horse was not the one he had had in Surrey, and commented upon it.

'We gave it back to Lord Osborne when we moved,' said

Charles, looking rather sad, 'but I do not much mind it. This one is got from the stables, because we have no room for a horse in our new home.'

'So you have moved – to Highgate?'

'Yes, and Uncle rode over to Croydon to see you yesterday, but the people told him you were gone.'

'Charles,' Mr Howard said, 'will you hold the horses' heads, while I walk a little way with Miss Emma?'

Charles assented with a very knowing look, and Emma suddenly found herself almost alone on the snowy heath with the man whom, an hour earlier, she had been struggling to dismiss from her thoughts for ever. She could not look up at him; she was entirely at a loss for words.

'Do take my arm,' Mr Howard said, 'it is rather rough underfoot.'

She complied, and they started off again in the Parliament Hill direction. For the first few minutes, she found it impossible to believe that she was actually walking next to him, tightly clasped to his side; a minute later, it seemed the most natural thing in the world. He cleared his throat a few times, commented on the beauty of the scenery, asked her more than once how she liked Hampstead. Her own responses were low and almost inaudible.

'I hardly know how to begin,' Mr Howard said, 'and I am afraid I did not express myself very clearly when we last met, but – Well, you will be aware that my connection with the Castle family has been oppressive to me for some time. The row with Osborne, when he had the impertinence to force his attentions on you, was merely the last straw.'

'You had a quarrel?' asked Emma.

'Oh, yes, a tremendous quarrel. I think I told you that I took the living, in the first place to provide for Harriet and her family, and also because I hoped to have some influence with Osborne – but it is long since I gave up expecting that. They were very kind, very liberal, but I was living in their grounds as a dependant, a companion to play cards with when they were bored. Well, I am not my namesake, the prison reformer, but I did wish to be useful.'

'I understand that very well.'

'I could do some limited good in the parish,' Mr Howard went on, 'but the truth is, Emma – Miss Watson – that I have long been seeking other employment. Harriet knows and approves. And at last I have my wish; I am appointed headmaster of a school in Highgate – not very far from here, as I said. Harriet is to be matron, and the boys will get a free education. I should greatly like to show you the place.'

'I am sure,' Emma said faintly, 'that you will make a success of it.'

'It is on a hilltop – very good air – a large house, plenty of room for the children to rattle around and they already like it. They will not have the luxuries they could have got from Osborne Castle, but we have what is much better, our independence.' He stopped and grasped her hands in his. 'I shall never be a rich man, Emma, but – will you take me on?'

Emma began to say – she knew not what, but the prolonged uncertainty of the last weeks had been too much for her and a sudden burst of weeping made her almost speechless. Mr Howard was greatly concerned, drying her tears with his glove and asking her repeatedly what he had done to distress her. At long last she was able to say, 'I was afraid – that I would never see you again.'

'Why, Emma – I thought you were aware when I left you at Croydon that I fully intended to come back. But I did not then have a home to offer you, and wished to have all clear and decided before speaking to your brother. You must have known I liked you, Emma?'

'I hoped -,' Emma confessed, wiping away her tears, 'but, Mr Howard -.'

'John.'

'John – was there never any affection between you and Lady Osborne?'

'Pooh, nothing of the sort,' Mr Howard said, turning very red. 'I can't believe she would have wished it, any more than I did, and we have not one thought or feeling in common besides.'

'I think she did wish it.'

Emma was fairly sure that he had been aware of Lady Osborne's feelings, although he would not say so, and that these had provided yet another motive for him to leave Wickstead for ever. She honoured him for not abusing the woman who had passionately, though injudiciously loved him, and resolved that her name should never be mentioned between them again. Whether the lady had hinted to Tom Musgrave that their marriage was a settled thing, intending him to pass on this news to herself, or whether Tom had merely been rattling on in his usual manner, now mattered very little.

'I am not such a coxcomb as to think so. But, my dearest Emma,' cried Mr Howard, 'how could you believe that, knowing *you*, with your beauty and goodness, I could conceivably be in love with Lady Osborne?'

'And how could you believe, that knowing *you*, I could be in love with her son?'

'Oh, I did not – I knew you had more sense – but it almost maddened me to hear Tom Musgrave, and then himself, talking as if it were a settled thing. They seemed to think that no girl, sensible or otherwise, would ever turn down a peer of the realm. If that empty-headed fellow had – well, I determined to come to Croydon and see for myself. And I really thought, at the time, that I had made my hopes and wishes very clear.'

Emma smiled, and did not reproach him. Even the kindest of men, she thought, could hardly conceive how a woman living at home, quiet and retired, could be prey to the most intense anxieties. The days which for her had passed so slowly had, for him, been filled with the business of winding up his life in Surrey and moving with Mrs Blake and the children to Highgate, and he had come to her as soon as he was free. They wandered across the snow for another quarter hour, too delighted with one another's company to know where they were heading. Mr Howard persisted in claiming that his feelings for her must always have been obvious. 'I think I began to love you when I first saw you dancing with Charles,' he said, 'and each time I have seen you since has only strengthened and deepened it. And here is a young man who wants to know what we are about.'

Charles, grown tired of waiting, had ridden up and cried: 'Uncle John! Has she said yes?'

'You little monkey,' Mr Howard said, dropping Emma's arm rather hastily, 'how did you *know*?'

'Oh, I saw how you looked at her, and how she looked at you. Are you going to marry him, Emma? My Mama hopes so, and you will have such a good time when you come to Highgate. We will go dancing together every week, and Uncle can sit on the side and play cards with the old people. Did you say yes, Emma?'

'Yes,' said Emma, and Charles immediately leapt off his mount and performed a jig in the snow, crying:

'I *told* you she was nicer than all the Osbornes!'

## *Chapter the Last*

THE FOLLOWING WEEK, Elizabeth and Purvis were married at Croydon, and three weeks later, and in the same church, Emma became the wife of Mr Howard.

It was a great pleasure to Robert Watson to give away his eldest and youngest sister, although, as his wife complained, they could much better have spared the other two. Soon, however, only one was left, for Mrs O'Brien, introduced to Margaret at the earlier wedding, had immediately in the warmth of her heart offered her Emma's room, as soon as Emma should have moved to Highgate School. For Margaret, this was a joyful release. She had stayed in Croydon for too long, had worn out all its pleasures and quarrelled with almost every member of her family, and having really a less bad disposition than Penelope, she was grateful for her aunt's kindness and anxious to make a fresh start in a more congenial neighbourhood. Mrs O'Brien was not disappointed. They joined the Book Society, painted water colours together, went to almost every dinner and dance and often drove across the heath to Emma's home, where Margaret was soon reporting that she had many admirers among the young men of Highgate and Hampstead.

Penelope remained in Croydon, more or less unhappily, with her brother and sister. Jane's nerves were slightly soothed by having most of her house to herself again, and the two women did not quarrel above once a month, although Mrs Robert was often heard to say it was a thousand pities, that Dr Harding had not lived one week more. Penelope herself said she did not envy either of her married sisters, and that she certainly could have had Purvis years ago, but had not wanted him. She was angered by the good terms on which he and Elizabeth lived together, and by her kindly relations with his children. Jane remarked that if Sam married Mary Edwards, as seemed likely, and set up his own house in Guildford, Penny could always go to live there and try her luck.

Emma sometimes worried that Captain O'Brien might return to disturb her aunt, but John made light of her fears. 'I shall keep a sharp eye on the India news,' he said, 'and if the scoundrel ever *does* turn up, he will find that he has a man to deal with this time.' Her happiness in her marriage was almost perfect, and she found in Mrs Blake a more affectionate sister than Penelope, Margaret or Jane, and in her children true friends.

Lady Osborne soon left the Castle, and did not return for several years. Too many people in Surrey suspected or knew of her infatuation with Mr Howard, whether because of her own rash conduct or Tom Musgrave's chatter, and when that young man called at the house in Wimpole Street, hoping to be asked to meet some people of fashion, he was informed that her ladyship was not at home. Her son, having killed all the birds on his estate, followed her to London, where most of his companions found him very stupid, apart, that is, from a number of young ladies, who professed that they dearly loved a lord. He was often to be seen at his club, complaining, after a pint of sherry, that he would never understand why the beautiful Emma Watson had joined her life to a man in every way inferior to himself – his own old tutor – and one who did not even like hunting – but, in spite of these deficiencies, it is certain that Emma never regretted her choice.

# POSTSCRIPT

Jane Austen probably wrote *The Watsons* around 1804, when she and her sister were living in Bath with their elderly parents and she was coming up to twenty-nine. She had already written *Northanger Abbey* and the early versions of *Sense and Sensibility* and *Pride and Prejudice,* but had been unable to publish them. Her career seemed blocked, her marriage prospects nil, and she knew that she would have to leave her home and become dependent on her brothers when Mr Austen died.

The fragment breaks off at the end of my Chapter 5, with the words 'the visitors departed without her'. Perhaps Austen stopped writing after the death of her father on 21st January 1805, because the last pages strongly suggest that the heroine's father will die very soon. She never took it up again, and she would not begin another novel for eight years.

Many of Jane Austen's legion of admirers have not read *The Watsons,* and it has sometimes been described as morbid and depressing. But it contains some of her most powerful writing, such as the conversation between Emma and Elizabeth about marriage, near the beginning, and Emma's meditations in her father's sickroom near the end. Call these depressing if you like; but the book also has a spirited heroine, a splendid ball scene, a great deal of quiet comedy and the most convincing child in all Jane Austen's fiction, little Charles. There are affinities with the two long novels she had already written. Emma and Elizabeth, like Elinor and Marianne, have no money to speak of and their relationship with their mercenary brother and his wife is not easy. Like the equally hard-up Jane and Elizabeth Bennet, they have two sisters who embarrass them by running after men. I believe that, if the plot is followed through, we shall also find something in common with *Mansfield Park*.

The manuscript was carefully kept in the family for over sixty years, and eventually published in 1871 in the second edition of the *Memoir of Jane Austen* by her nephew, J.E. Austen-Leigh. He added this note:

'When the author's sister, Cassandra, showed the manuscript of this work to some of her nieces, she also told them something of the intended story; for with this dear sister – though, I believe, with no one else – Jane seems to have talked freely of any work she might have in hand. Mr Watson was soon to die; and Emma to become dependent for a home on her narrow-minded sister-in-law and brother. She was to decline an offer of marriage from Lord Osborne, and much of the interest of the tale was to arise from Lady Osborne's love for Mr Howard, and his counter affection for Emma, whom he was finally to marry.'

Some of this can be deduced from the existing manuscript. Emma's father will die, though not before she has got to know more of Mr Howard and the Osbornes, and she and her sisters will move to Croydon. There will be family tensions and they will be expected to accept any proposal they get. Lord Osborne's interest in Emma is already obvious; I suspect that this character was inspired by a young man whom Jane, two years earlier, had refused to marry. He was not a lord, just a plain Mr Harris Bigg-Wither, but he was rich, though uncouth, and could have given her a luxurious home. Her decision to turn him down, after a night of agonising, must have seemed foolish to many people, and we can be sure that the arguments for and against marrying for security would have been important in the finished novel. Mr Howard, although he says nothing in the fragment, is the poorer but more interesting man whom Emma can love.

But 'Lady Osborne's love for Mr Howard' – is this possible? He is 'a little more than thirty', she is 'nearly fifty'. Jane's first editor, R.W. Chapman, believed that she had been confused with her daughter *Miss* Osborne, who is obviously a more suitable age for a bride. But I disagree, for three reasons. First, because people of Jane Austen's time did not confuse Miss and Lady, any more than my generation confused Mrs and Miss. Second, because the Austen family had no doubt that Lady Osborne was the person meant. And finally, because there is quite strong internal evidence that it was indeed the older woman whom the author had in mind. We are told that she is 'very handsome' and has 'by much the finest person' of the women in her group, although all of them are younger. This is no sweet old dowager but a woman who has by no means given up on the opposite sex. We also hear a lot about Emma's forty-something aunt, who has caused a scandal by getting married again. Jane Austen had already written *Lady Susan,* about a wicked, glamorous widow of thirty-five who outshines her own daughter and has an electric effect on men. Perhaps the character owes something to her fascinating cousin Eliza, who had married first a French aristocrat and then Jane's brother Henry, who was fully ten years younger than herself.

So, without too much straining, we can imagine how the story might have developed. Mr Howard, like Mr Collins, is a clergyman living in the shadow of the local great house and is on friendly terms with his patrons, who constantly invite him to dine and play cards with them. Being a sensible man, unlike Mr Collins, he would have no illusions about the family and might find this relationship oppressively close. But his sister who lives with him is a widow with four children, probably dependent on him, so he might not find it very easy to get away. He and Emma (like Edmund and Fanny in *Mansfield Park)* are a virtuous couple who are sought in marriage by a richer and more worldly pair, the Osbornes. These marriages will not come off because the moral, hard-working middle class to which Jane Austen's family belonged and the effete aristocracy do not mix. After such a crisis, I thought it unlikely that the two households could go on being friends. The Howards, Blakes and Osbornes have a cosy relationship in the existing novel, but in the end, Mr Howard and his new wife will have to go elsewhere.

There are other questions which Jane Austen never answered. Will Penelope and Margaret find husbands? Will Sam get Mary Edwards with her ten thousand pounds and will Elizabeth get over her first love, Purvis? What is the role of Tom Musgrave, who does not seem to be a suitable husband for anybody? Will Emma's aunt ever reappear? Some characters have not been introduced at all, and others have not spoken a word, so if anyone is bold enough to try to finish this novel, there is plenty of work for them. No one can know exactly what Jane Austen would have done, but when I decided to have a go, I determined that I would stay within her guidelines, and would not bring in any major new characters.

I guessed that other people might have written continuations, but had not read any of them except Joan Aiken's amusing *Emma Watson* (1996), which strays a very long way from the original. My own version was already written before I found that the book had first been completed as long ago as 1850, by Jane Austen's own niece. Catherine Hubback (1818-77), the daughter of Jane's sailor brother Frank, was an intelligent woman who was forced to become a self-supporting novelist when her husband had a mental breakdown, leaving her with three little boys to bring up. She had been too young to know her famous aunt but she did know Jane's sister Cassandra, who lived until 1845, very well. *The Watsons* had often been read aloud in the family circle and if anybody knew what was going to happen next, it would have been Cassandra and, through her, her niece.

These two women were much closer to Jane Austen in time, and in their ways of thinking, than I could be; Catherine's novel, *The Younger Sister*, might provide valuable clues.

This novel is long out of print and can only be read in the great libraries, but some of it has been used in another version of *The Watsons*, published in 1977. Catherine did not have her aunt's manuscript in front of her and rewrote the story from memory – proving that she knew it very well. Her novel is long and melodramatic, and introduces several characters who are not in Jane Austen, but her interpretation of the relationship between Osborne Castle and Wickstead Parsonage is essentially the same as mine. Emma soon becomes friendly with Mr Howard and his sister who, as she points out, 'are in our rank of life, though their intimacy at the Castle gives them an artificial consequence'. Mrs Blake is unhappy with this 'intimacy' and worries about Lady Osborne's interest in her brother:

'I should be glad if you had a living in some other part of the country... the inhabitants of the castle are almost too near to be pleasant. We are under obligations which neither party can forget... You have no idea how exacting she is; and if my brother were not one of the best-tempered men in the world we never could go on as well as we do.'

*(The Younger Sister,* Volume 1, Chapter 8)

Mr Howard is placed in a painful position when he realises that Lady Osborne is in love with him:

'Most unwelcome this conviction certainly was, as it could end, he thought, in nothing but a positive rupture between his family and the Osbornes; and unless he had the power of obtaining another home, it would certainly render them exceedingly uncomfortable. He knew the dowager to be of a vindictive disposition when she considered herself injured or insulted, and both to his own family, and that of his beloved Emma, he foresaw nothing but evil from the prospect before them. If Emma should accept the son, the rage of his mother would certainly be intense, and if she refused him and accepted Mr Howard instead, there was but little probability she would be better pleased. All hopes of further advancement from the family patronage would be at an end, and he was not sure that upon the small income his present living afforded him, it would be prudent to marry, as his sister and her little boy were quite dependent on himself. There were Charles's maintenance at a public school, and his subsequent expenses at the university to be looked forward to and provided for; he had engaged to do this, voluntarily engaged himself, and now that he came seriously to reflect on his position and ties, on the expenses of a married man, and the probabilities of any better future provision, he began to wonder what infatuation had before closed his eyes, and hurried him on against his better judgment, to an affection which threatened so much of care and difficulty. Yet it was hard, very hard, to give up the charming hopes with which he had flattered his fancy; he did not feel equal to such a sacrifice; he did not feel positively called to it.'

(*The Younger Sister,* Volume 2, Chapter 4)

Here is a very clear statement of the problems which Emma and Mr Howard are likely to face; Catherine, like her aunt, understood the realities of money and power. In her book, Lord Osborne is much nicer than in mine – though just as stupid – and the Robert Watsons rather worse. She and I both thought that Lady Osborne would turn out to be an unpleasant woman (*The Younger Sister* gives her 'dangerous fits' and 'vehement emotions'), and there were other startling similarities too. Emma's brother and his wife make Emma so unhappy that she thinks of getting a job as a governess; there is even the detail that Jane has sacked her nursemaid so she can make her sisters-in-law do her work. The aunt leaves her Irish husband, but keeps her income (unlikely, I thought, before the Married Women's Property Act). Mr Howard is assured that, if he marries Lady Osborne, he could become a bishop, which speaks volumes about the connection between the Church of England and the ruling classes in Jane Austen's world. In *The Younger Sister,* Lord Osborne kindly gives him another living so that he can get away; I preferred to have him find a job for himself. Irene Collins, in *Jane Austen and the Clergy* (1993), says that around ten per cent of clergymen dropped out and went into teaching, so it looked like a possible way out.

Was it presumptuous to 'finish' a Jane Austen novel which would surely have been a masterpiece if she had finished it herself? Yes, of course, but I believed that more people were likely to read it if they could find out 'what happened next'. I tried to work in Jane Austen's spirit and write the ending which she would probably have wanted, and it was encouraging to find that Catherine, her niece, had interpreted her mind in a very similar way.

*Merryn Williams*

## Notes

Page 1 - *The first winter assembly in the town of D. in Surrey.* Most country towns held an assembly once a month, around the time of the full moon so that people could get home in the light. The young men and women danced while the older ones sat on the side and played cards. The town of D. is thought to be Dorking; R. is Reigate.

Page 4 - *Dr Harding.* Chichester is a cathedral city, and I think that it is likely that Dr Harding is not a physician but a cleric, like Dr Grant in *Mansfield Park*. Medical men, like Sam, had a rather low social position in Jane Austen's world.

Page 64 - *who has the living of Alford about fourteen miles off.* This sentence was crossed out of Jane Austen's manuscript, and indicates that Purvis is a clergyman.